Anonymous

Dover, New Hampshire

its history and industries descriptive of the city and its manufacturing and business

interests. Issued as an illustrated souvenir in commemoration of the twenty-fifth

anniversary of Foster's Daily Democrat

Anonymous

Dover, New Hampshire
its history and industries descriptive of the city and its manufacturing and business interests. Issued as an illustrated souvenir in commemoration of the twenty-fifth anniversary of Foster's Daily Democrat

ISBN/EAN: 9783337405816

Printed in Europe, USA, Canada, Australia, Japan

Cover: Foto ©Andreas Hilbeck / pixelio.de

More available books at **www.hansebooks.com**

DOVER, NEW HAMPSHIRE,

ITS HISTORY AND INDUSTRIES

ISSUED AS AN

ILLUSTRATED SOUVENIR

IN COMMEMORATION OF THE

TWENTY-FIFTH ANNIVERSARY

OF

FOSTER'S DAILY DEMOCRAT

DESCRIPTIVE OF THE CITY AND ITS MANUFACTURING
AND BUSINESS INTERESTS.

COMPILED BY A. E. G. NYE.

CONTAINING:

Concise History; Old Landmarks; Present and Former Residents; Its Institutions; Buildings;
Picturesque Scenes; Comfortable Homes; Portraits and Biographical Sketches of
Active Men; Men noted in Public, Business and Professional Life;
Its Manufacturing and Commerce; Statements of Resources
and Advantages of Locality; Its Growth, Pros-
perity and Future Possibilities.

PUBLISHED BY
GEO. J. FOSTER & CO.
1893.

Introduction.

IN the publication of this book, with a view to the welfare of the community, Foster's Daily Democrat presents its compliments to its thousands of readers on the twenty-fifth anniversary of its birth. Great care has been exercised in the preparation of this work, and it is to be trusted that a perusal of its pages will prove it to be a work wider in scope and different in character from anything ever before published in this city.

GEORGE J. FOSTER & CO.,
Publishers.

BIRDS-EYE VIEW OF DOVER FROM GARRISON HILL.

ON a spring day in 1623, a vessel, name of which is now lost, landed upon the western shore of the Piscataqua, two parties sent out by the company of Laconia. One party, consisting of Edward and William Hilton (brothers), with a few other persons, took possession of

Possibly other settlers came over in the years immediately following 1623 ; but, in 1631, there were only three houses in all that part of the Piscataqua. In that year Captain Thomas Wiggin was sent over by the patentees ; in 1632 he returned to England, and in 1633 he came back with

THE CITY HALL.

the beautiful neck of land lying between the Newichawannock and Bellamy rivers, some six miles up the Piscataqua ; and, with the necessaries which they had brought with them, began the settlement, which, in 1639, received the name of Dover; in 1640, that of Northam ; and, in 1641, that of Dover again, which it has since borne.

"about thirty settlers," some of whom were " of good estate and some account for religion," and others of no particular account for either. These settlers, landing at Salem, from the ship *James*, October 10, 1633, proceeded immediately to Dover, and took up small lots upon Dover Neck, "where they intended to build a compact town." Captain Wiggin, by authority from the owners in England, distributed these lots, recorded the titles,

transacted the company's business generally, and "had the power of a governor hereabouts." In the same band came Rev. William Leverich, "an able and worthy Puritan minister." The inhabitants immediately erected a meeting-house;

REV. HANSERD KNOLLYS.

trading post. He himself became major, commander of the New Hampshire forces, counsellor, acting president of the province, chief justice, representative, and speaker of the Massachusetts general court.

From 1633 to 1641, Dover, although increasing in population, experienced a succession of troubles. The original settlers were Episcopalians; those of 1633 Puritans. To these discordant elements was added the bad character of some men, who, forced to leave Massachusetts, acquired influence in this loose society. The ill results soon appeared. Mr. Leverich was forced to leave in 1635 for want of

DOVER, FROM THE SITE OF FIRST MEETING HOUSE.

and, with the tan pits, and other means of practical crafts which soon followed, Dover began its organized existence.

In addition to the original purposes of the settlement (fishing), trade with the Indians and the manufacture of lumber soon followed. Both of these were mainly in connection with the settlement of Richard Walderne (whose descendants bear the name of Waldron), in 1640, or a little earlier, at the lower falls of the Cochecho, where the compact part of the present city of Dover stands. He built a saw-mill, and soon after a grist-mill; and, for half a century, his house was a frontier

support. Rev. George Burdett, who succeeded him in 1637, was able, ambitious, unscrupulous, and profligate; but, before his character became known, he prevailed upon the people to make him governor; but, soon exposing himself, he fled to Agamenticus. In the ministry he was succeeded by Hanserd Knollys, a good and pious

DR. JEREMY BELKNAP.

man ; and by him the first church in Dover was organized, in December, 1638. The first meeting-house in Dover was erected in 1634 or earlier, and stood near the Beck Cove, on the western slope of the Neck. The second was built on the spot where the remnant of the fortifications once around it still remains. This house was standing in a ruinous state in 1720. The second meeting-house was probably built a little after the year 1700, for Mr. Sever, who was settled in 1711, and dismissed in 1715, preached in both

The remainder of the house was subsequently taken down. The fourth and present meeting-house was erected in 1829, and cost about $12,000. The parish was incorporated as a parish district from the town by an act of the Provincial Assembly.

Jeremy Belknap D.D., eleventh minister, was distinguished for his literary attainments and beloved for his personal character. He was an ardent patriot in the Revolution, and by his writings and correspondence did eminent service. He

WHITCHER'S FALLS ON COCHECO RIVER.

houses. This house was sold in 1759 and taken down the following year. It stood on Pine Hill, on land now inclosed in the burying-ground, very near its northern boundary, and a little west of north of the tomb of the Cushing family. The third edifice erected in 1758, stood where the present house stands. In 1829, the parish voted to sell the old meeting-house. The northern end was taken off and converted by the purchaser into a dwelling house, and now stands on the east side of Court Street, near the brook.

published numerous works, the best known of which is his " History of New Hampshire."

In civil office Burdett was followed by Captain John Underhill, an old European soldier and a refugee from Massachusetts, having a strange mixture of enthusiasm, ability, and hypocrisy. Underhill was deposed in 1640 for various crimes. Knollys was eclipsed by the superior talents of Thomas Larkham, an emigrant of 1639 or 1640, and forced to yield. The discordant elements now broke out into disgraceful contests, ended at last by the union of Dover with Massachusetts, Oct. 9, 1641, which the better

tory it embraced, in addition to its present limits, Durham, Madbury, Lee, Somersworth, Rollinsford, and part of Newington,

BLOODY POINT.

—all of which were included in Dover in 1641, when its boundaries were defined for the first time, and all of which were settled before 1660. In civil affairs it enjoyed virtual self-government. The only disturbance was that caused by the royal commissioners in 1665, who en-

part of the people adopted as the only cure for their difficulties. It was gladly welcomed by the latter power, who, indeed, claimed a latent right to the territory by virtue of their own patent. The town was made part of old Norfolk county, was represented in the general court, and was subject to the laws of Massachusetts until New Hampshire, in 1679, was erected into a separate province.

From 1641 to 1679 Dover had generally peace, ecclesiastically and civilly. The Massachusetts government bore lightly, and the clergymen were able and excellent men. The only jar in religious matters was that caused by the coming of Quakerism, in 1662, and the barbarous sentence upon women of ten lashes upon the naked back. Of course Quakerism flourished with greater vigor in Dover than in any other town in the province. In business the town increased, having a direct trade with the West Indies, exporting principally lumber. In population it gained rapidly for a time ; the tax-paying males increasing from 54 in 1648 to 142 in 1659, and 155 in 1668. It then experienced a check, falling to 146 in 1675, doubtless on account of the Indian wars. In terri-

deavored to find or create a public sentiment in opposition to the government of Massachusetts Bay ; but, so far as Dover was concerned, entirely in vain. A greater cause of disturbance was the occasional efforts of the heirs of Mason to establish their pro-

OLD FRANKLIN ACADEMY.

SCENE ON THE COCHECO RIVER.

prietary claims, efforts which developed themselves more fully at a later period.

During this period some town votes are worthy of copying. One was that of the 27th of November, 1648, when " It is this [day] ordered at publique Town meeting that Richard Pinkame shall beate the drumme on Lord's days to give notice for the time of meeting." This method continued for several years. In 1665 it was " Ordered that mr. Petter Coffin shall be Impowered by this meitting to A Gree with some workman to Build a Terrett upon the meeitting house for to hang

the Bell wich wee have Bought of Capt. Walldern." In 1657 " Charles Buckner chosen by voet A Scoellmaster for this town." Other schoolmasters followed, among whom, early in the next century, was " Master Sullefund " (Sullivan), ancestor of the eminent family of that name. In 1653 the second meeting-house was built, which was " forty foot longe, twenty-six foote wide, sixteen foote studd, with six windows, two doores fitt for such a house, with a tile covering, and to planck all the walls, with glass and nails for it." The third church was built in 1714 (whose bell was hung on a schoolhouse near by) ; the fourth in 1758, which last was used

until 1828. From 1679 to the close of the Indian wars Dover suffered extremely. Population, it is true, largely increased during the latter part of the period ; thus the number of polls in 1675 was 131, and in 1727, 466 (Newington in both cases being excluded). Nor did any ecclesiastical troubles occur, beyond the efforts of the present town of Durham to obtain separate authority, in which they succeeded in 1716 ; and the question whether the proper site for a place of worship was not at Cochecho, instead of Dover Neck, which question was settled in 1711 by having the meetings alternate, and, in 1720, by the entire removal to the newer but far larger place. But the Indian wars severely

THE OLD GARRISON HOUSES.

impaired, for a long series of years, the prosperity of the place.

It was a frontier town, touching the forests which stretched away to Canada, defending an extensive frontier, and possessing but a scattered population. In addition to the general causes of Indian hostility, in their own jealousy and the machinations of the French, local differences had grown out of trading operations. Suspicions of hostility had been so far excited, as early as 1667, as to lead, at that time, to the fortification of the meeting-house, by " intrenchments and flankarts,"

ON LOCUST STREET.

in whose inclosure sentinels paced during divine service, and whose ruins are still visible. On the breaking out of the general war of 1675, there commenced a series of attacks upon the inhabitants, which, with occasional and sometimes protracted intervals of peace, did not wholly end until the treaty of Aix-la-Chapelle. As most of these were petty affairs, and of the same general character, it is unnecessary to narrate them particularly. Exposed houses were captured and burned, individuals at work were killed; inhabitants were waylaid and shot on their way to church; captives were carried to Canada, to be ransomed at a heavy expense, or, in repeated cases, to live and die there, where the blood of Dover settlers is still perpetuated. On the other hand, Indians were often surprised; their stores of provisions were destroyed; the woods were scoured by rangers, especially by parties of exasperated young men; and sometimes severe blows were struck. The most destructive affair, upon what is now Dover soil, may be more particularly noticed.

It occurred on the morning of the 28th of June, 1689. Thirteen years before, at a time when, although war had broken out on the Kennebec, there was peace at Piscataqua, 400 Indians were assembled at Cochecho, 200 of whom were refugees from the south of Massachusetts; and, ignorant of the unity of the government, thought themselves safe with Major Wal-

derne, who then commanded the forces of that territory. Two companies of whites, on their way to the Kennebec, stopped at Dover, who brought with them orders to seize all Indians recently hostile, which they would have proceeded by force to obey; but Walderne, knowing the bloodshed which would follow, dissuaded them, and contrived a stratagem to seize them by means of a sham fight. It was successful; the whole were disarmed, and the Southern Indians were sent to Boston, where four or five were hung, and the remainder sold into slavery. Thirteen years passed away, during which a relentless thirst for vengeance was cherished. In the course of this period former habits of trade revived, and whites and Indians ming'ed freely. But the old enmity was fostered by some of those enslaved who had returned. On the

DR. EZRA GREEN, AT 101 YEARS OF AGE.

27th of June, the Indians were noticed to be gathered in unaccustomed numbers. Many strange faces also appeared. Some of the people hinted to Walderne their suspicions. "Go plant your pumpkins, and I will tell you when the Indians will break out," was his merry reply. That evening, a young man told him that the town was full of Indians. "I know the Indians very well," said Walderne, "and there is no danger." The Indians told him that a number of Indians were coming to trade next day. "Brother Walderne," said Messandowitt, as they sat at supper, "what would you do if the strange Indians should come?" "I could assemble a hundred men by lifting up my finger," was his careless answer. In the evening two squaws applied at each garrison house (Walderne's Heard's, Otis's, Paine's, the two Coffins', and Gerrish's), for permission to sleep before the kitchen fire, as had often been done before. It was granted at Walderne's, Heard's, the elder Coffin's and Otis's. In the hour of deepest quiet the doors were opened: the Indians in waiting entered. Walderne, though seventy-four years old, defended himself with vigor until stunned by a blow on the back of his head. The Indians then dragged him into the hall, placed him in his chair upon the table, with a derisive cry, "who shall judge Indians now?" and cut him across the breast in turn, each exclaiming, "I cross out my account," and finally killed him. A messenger sent from Bos-

ton with warning of this very attack was delayed a night at Newbury. When he reached Cochecho the next morning, he found four or five houses burned, four garrisons destroyed, twenty-three persons killed, and that twenty-nine were captives on their way to Canada. Among these was Christine Otis, whose romantic adventures a limited space forbids us to recount. Other attacks were made upon parts of what was then Dover, disastrous still, but the intrepid settlers never fell back for a day from their frontier position. Among the various arts to surprise the whites, tradition has preserved the following: The haymakers, having made hay upon a meadow a mile or more up the river from the falls, had piled it into cocks and left it. One warm day, when the men were absent from Walderne's garrison (a few rods from the lower falls), and the doors were open for air, the women noticed the haycocks floating down the stream. They exclaimed against this wanton mischief; but none, save one, paid any further attention to it; and she, as she sat carelessly looking, was suddenly surprised to see the cocks edging towards the shore. A close inspection revealed the cause—under every haycock an Indian was swimming. She gave the alarm; the doors were hastily closed, and the house secured just in time against the baffled savages.

In the midst of other troubles, the Masonian controversy revived. Several cases were tried at Dover in 1683, Wald-

BRACEWELL BLOCK, BEFORE THE FLOOD.

derne's being the first. He made no defense, asserted no title, and gave no evidence. Judgment was entered against him, and other cases followed; but in no case could an execution be enforced. Riots ensued, the attempt to enforce an execution at Dover being ended by a woman's knocking down the officer with a bible. Against such a spirit nothing could be done, and the suits were suspended. They again came up in 1703, pased through various courts, and were a source of constant perplexity to the peo-

ple, and g r e a t complication i n political affairs, until 1746.

From the con-clusion of the In-dian wars to the Revolution, noth-ing peculiar marks t h e history of Dover. Its busi-n e s s (including s h i p b u i l ding) continued to increase. Its population in 1767 was 1,614, having already lost Mad-bury and Somersworth (including Rollins-ford), Durham, and Lee. The population of the original territory at that time was 5,446; of the present Dover 1,666, in-cluding twenty-six slaves. During the Revolution it bore its part of the burdens, supplying largely both troops and money. An entire regiment was enlisted at Dover by Colonel John Waldron, under whom it joined the army at Cambridge. The town itself paid bounties to all who enlisted.

BRACEWELL BLOCK, AFTER THE FLOOD.

All through the war, in Rhode Island, at Bennington, at Saratoga, at New York, and on every field where northern troops were found, Dover men were in active service; while at sea, not a few of its hardy sons were the followers of John Paul Jones. The last person known to have served with him, Dr. Ezra Green, surgeon on board the *Ranger*, died in Dover, July 27, 1847, aged 101 years and one month, being previous to his death the oldest living graduate of Harvard College.

From the close of the war of the Revo-lution until the introduction of cotton manufacturing, the town grew somewhat slowly. Its population in 1790 was 1,998;

in 1800, 2,062; in 1810, 2,228; in 1820, 2,871, which by 1860 had increased to 8,186, the valuation at that time being $3,629,442. It was, so far, a farming and ship-building town. But, with the erection of cotton mills a change came over the place. The succession of saw-mills, grist-mills, fulling-mills, oil-mills, and nail factory, which had covered 181 years ended in 1821, when the "Dover Factory Company" was incorporated, by which, and its successor, the "Cocheco Manu-facturing Company," the present large cotton factories and print works were erected. To this enterprise alone must be ascribed the steady growth and commercial prosperity of Dover.

In 1841 the opening of the Boston and Maine railroad, and the construction, a few years after, of the Cocheco railroad to Alton, to both of which Dover people contributed liberally, had a marked effect upon the business of the town. While its local trade and interests were on the increase, its importance as a distributing point for interior trade declined. The Dover-Packet Company, which had for

superseded by a city organization. With the city government came in the use of gas in lighting the streets and dwellings, improved sidewalks, a police court, a more efficient administration of the laws, and other city institutions, quiet and orderly elections included. The act incorporating the City of Dover was signed June 29, 1855, and was accepted by the citizens at a town meeting held August 15, 1855. The first mayor, Andrew Peirce, took the oath of office March 25, 1856, and the city government was then inaugurated.

VIEW ON SILVER STREET.

many years given life and activity to the wharves and storehouses on the river, soon discharged its last cargo, the Landing ceased to be the centre of business, which from this time gathered around the railroad station and the streets leading to it. In 1847 the introduction of shoe manufacturing for the southern and western markets added largely to the business of the place, employing after a few years a large capital, and in a good season more workmen than any other industry.

In 1855 the town government, after an existence of 222 years, or from 1633, was

During the Civil war the part borne by the Dover companies has emblazoned their names on the scroll of fame. On the evening of the President's first call the citizens met in the city hall. The mayor, Alphonso Bickford, presided, and resolutions were unanimously adopted, commending the President's action and pledging their support to the government. Companies were formed and the patriotism of the citizens was unbounded. On Wednesday, April 17th, 1861, by authority of the Governor of the State, George W. Colbath opened a recruiting-office in our City Hall. On Thursday he informed the Governor that the first company was full. He was directed to proceed with enlistments. On the next Monday 150 men were on the muster roll. On Monday, the 29th, the first two companies were to leave home, to become Companies A and B of the First New Hampshire. The day before they had listened to a stirring sermon in the old First Church, from a successor of that minister who had preached to the soldiers here on the same spot as they were to take up their march to Cambridge in 1775. At ten o'clock,

11th of May the choice was given to each, —three years or be discharged. Seventy-one on that day chose the three years, and five days afterwards the number was 104. On the 25th that company left the city to become company D in the gallant second New Hampshire.

Of how many men this city furnished during the four years that followed the record is not perfect. Even in the imperfect rolls there were Dover men in each of the first fifteen regiments and in the eighteenth, in the cavalry, the navy, and the marine corps. From the call of July

CENTRAL AVENUE, LOOKING SOUTH.

Monday morning, they were in line in Central Square, 145 men in the ranks. Four thousand people witnessed the scene, —in the streets, from windows, from balconies, from the house-tops. The women had been working day by day to supply needed clothing, some of them whose tears dropped as they sewed. Prayer was offered by one who soon after himself went to serve in the navy, Rev. T. G. Salter.

A third company was meanwhile formed from the excess of enlistments. Orders now came, however, to receive only those who would enlist for three years. On the

2nd, 1862, 582 names are on record. Prior to that were all the first men of the first eight regiments, and of the sailors entering the navy before that date which should be added. Some examination of the rolls shows that more than 800 enlistments were made by this city of 8,500 inhabitants. Dover men served in the Shenandoah and in the first disastrous march to Bull Run; they were in the Peninsula battles and marches; in the several battles before Washington; in the bloody charge at Antietam bridge. They were in the charge up the heights of St.

Marie. They were in the burning woods of Chancellorsville. They were where Lee hurled his legions against Cemetery Hill at Gettysburg; in the long and bloody march from the Wilderness to Petersburg. They were in North Carolina. They were with Burnside in Tennessee, and with Sherman back of Vicksburg, and they sailed the coast, and watched the harbors, and manned the war boats on the Mississippi.

To raise and put its quota of men into the service, under the various calls which were issued, the city advanced upwards of $250,000, increasing its expenditures from $59,272, in 1860, to $233,462 in 1865. A soldiers' monument was erected in the Pine Hill burying-ground by Charles W. Sawyer Post, G. A. R., and dedicated Sept. 17, 1877.

In 1871 Congress appropriated $10,000 for the purpose of removing obstructions in the Cocheco River. In 1872 an additional sum of $10,000 was granted, followed by a like amount in each of the two succeeding years.

THE HIGH SCHOOL.

In 1875 the sum was increased to $25,000, and later a further sum of $15,000, which gave free access to vessels employed in the coal and other freighting business upon the river.

In November, 1872, ground was broken for the construction of the Portsmouth and Dover Railroad, an enterprise which had been in contemplation for more than twenty years. The road was built in that and the following year, and opened for travel in February, 1874, costing some $800,000, of which sum the city, in its municipal capacity contributed $258,000,

while many of its citizens made liberal private subscriptions for stock.

The "Dover Building Association" was organized in March, 1875, with a capital of $10,000. Since that time it has invested between $30,000 and $40,000 in real estate, building about thirty dwelling-houses, many of which have already been satisfactorily disposed of, affording handsome dividends to the stockholders, and furnishing desirable tenements to a most valuable class of population.

On the morning of March 22, 1889, the old city hall was completely destroyed by fire, which also damaged the spire of the Belknap church adjoining. The damage in all amounted to $100,000. The county and city had been joint occupants of the building, and after its destruction Rochester endeavored to obtain the new county building which then became necessary, but it was decided to retain the County seat in Dover, and the present handsome building on Second street was erected. Immediately after the fire, steps were taken to build another city hall and the present site was chosen. The lot faces on Central avenue and is bounded by Locust, Hale, and St. Thomas streets. It formerly contained the St. Thomas church, and old Lafayette house the former of which was demolished and the latter removed across the street. The city sold the old site upon which now stands the Masonic Temple. The corner stone of the present city hall was laid July 4th, 1890, and the new building dedicated December 16, 1891. The plans were drawn by George G. Adams, of Lawrence, Mass., and the contractors were McIntyre and Abbott who subsequently sub-let the brick-work to Mack Bros., of Salem, Mass. The building was however finished by the Building Committee consisting of Hon. B. Frank Nealley, Chairman ; John Holland, Joshua L. Foster, Dennis Cash, Joseph T. Woodbury, Charles M. Corson and Nathaniel C. Wentworth.

March 1, 1896, will long be remembered by the citizens of Dover as the "night of the flood." Considerable damage was done to property. Six bridges within the city's limits were demolished ; four

away in the distance, views may be had of uncommon beauty. The Newichawannock, the Bellamy and Cochecho, which flow through the city in a southeast direction, not only add to its beauty, but also to its wealth, by their direct and navigable connection with the ocean. The city is rich in historic land-marks ; old residences, churches, business blocks and relics of the past are to be seen on every hand. But these have become very much obscured by the palpable evidences of improvement and progress everywhere throughout the city, especially in the residential sections.

STRAFFORD GUARDS ON THE WAY TO THE FRONT.

stores with all their stock were swept away, including the southern end of the Bracewell block and the Central avenue bridge.

The situation of Dover is exceedingly pleasant. Gentle elevations, easy swells of land, and winding streams, characterize its surface. From the high ridge between the rivers Newichawannock and Bellamy, and from another elevation overlooking the waters of Great Bay with the Winnicumet, the Lamprey, the Swamscott, the Shaukhassick, and the Newichawannock (with its tributary the Cochecho), all uniting to form the Piscataqua, rolling

The Strafford Guards.

COMPANY F. FIRST REGIMENT NEW HAMP-
SHIRE VOLUNTEERS.

At no period since the stirring times of 1861-65 has the patriotism of Dover people reached such a height as when the President called for 125,000 volunteers to fight for the honor of our flag in our war with Spain. The Strafford Guards was the company chosen to go to the front, and on Saturday, May 7th, they left Dover amid scenes of wild enthusiasm and went into camp at Concord, 82 officers and

THE STRAFFORD GUARDS IN CAMP AT CONCORD, MAY, 1898.

men strong. Their departure was witnessed by thousands of citizens, and the city was gaily decorated, the Sawyer-Rifles and C. W. Sawyer Post, G. A. R. forming an escort to the depot. On May 12th, they were mustered into the United States service, and on the 17th departed for Chickamauga Park, Georgia, where they were stationed when this work went to press.

The Strafford Guards were permanently organized at Dover, in October, 1822, and in the spring of the next year the company became a part of the state militia, being

April 24, 1864, the company was mustered into the service of the United States for the period of sixty days and sent to Fort Constitution, New Castle, to assist in relieving the First Company New Hampshire Volunteer Heavy Artillery, which had been ordered to the front. On July 28, 1864, it was mustered out of the United States service. The company became Company A, Second Regiment New Hampshire Volunteer State Militia on September 26, 1866. During the year ending May 1878, the First and Second

COMMISSIONED AND NON-COMMISSIONED OFFICERS, STRAFFORD GUARDS.

styled the First Company Light Infantry, Second Regiment, Second Brigade, Second Division, New Hampshire Volunteer State Militia. During the summer of 1824, the company acted as escort to the Marquis de Lafayette, on the occasion of his visit to Dover. The Company was incorporated under the name of the Strafford Guards by act of the Legislature, approved June 27, 1835. On May 5, 1864, in pursuance of telegraphic instructions from Major-General John A. Dix, commanding the Department of the East, dated

Regiments were re-organized, and the Strafford Guards became Company A, First Regiment New Hampshire National Guard and continued so until recently when it became Company F. The company has several times been one of those selected to represent New Hampshire at celebrations in other states.

The roster of the company in camp at Concord, was as follows :—Captain, Frank E. Rollins ; First Lieutenant, Frank H. Keenan ; Second Lieutenant, Lewis E. Tuttle ; First Sergeant, John J. Gailey ;

Quartermaster Sergeant, Herbert C. Grime; Second Sergeant, John Sunderland; Third Sergeant, Joseph T. Cronin; Fourth Sergeant, Frank F. Davis; Fifth Sergeant, Joseph Connell; Corporals, John R. Maloney, Frank E. Russ, Edgar M. Foss, Cassius B. Roberts, Alexander J. McCabe, James McNally; Artificer, Austin E. Sanborn; Wagoner, John P. Miniter; Musicians, John B. Hebert and William Rossiter; Privates, Nelson E. Averill, William Boudreau, Oliver Boudreau, Harry E. Brooks, John Burley, Ben. R. Canney, John Canney, John E. Carroll, Ralph R. Cochrane (Somersworth), Wm. Connell (Rochester), Edward W. Cordes, Wm. J. Cormier (Somersworth), James Costello (Manchester), James J. Cronin (Manchester), John R. Curran (Somersworth), Edward Doherty, Hugh Donnelly, Jos. Drouin, James F. Duffy, Thos. Duffy, Pearl Foss, Frank H. Glidden, Owen E. Hanratty, R. Arnold Hill, Herbert B. Houghton (Warner), Henry Hughes, Fred O. Jackson, Ignace Jean (Nashua), John Kidney, Amay Lamire (Rochester), Pearlie E. Leach (Somersworth), Frank Lique (Rochester), Wm. J. Mahoney, George Marquis and Emil Marquis (Nashua), John T. McDonald, Hugh E. McDonald (Nashua), John J. McCooey, Arthur H. Merchant, Chr. Morley, Owen J. Mooney, Edward M. Murphy, Frank O. Mason, Arthur M. Pingree (Rochester), Carroll E. Pinkham, Alric W. Ramsey, James Rodden, John W. Rogers, Frank A. Rowe (Concord), Joseph W. Savoie, Almon H. Stewart (Rochester), Fred W. Steuerwald, James Sunderland, Frank H. Swain, Ralph G. Tanner (Rochester), Albert A. Taylor, Michael J. Trainor, Clarence R. Tuttle, Wm. G. Webber, Clarence H. Whitehouse, Irving L. Whitehouse, George W. Willey (Somersworth) and Henry R. Wood.

The company is composed of men of excellent physique who have been inured to work which eminently fits them for their arduous duties in the field. During their stay in camp at Concord their high state of discipline and their excellent conduct won for them golden opinions. The same is true of them at Camp Thomas, Chickamauga, where despite the extreme heat and the many privations incidental

to the massing at short notice of such a large number of troops, their discipline has been excellent. Constant drills, field manoeuvring, tactics and sentry duty have imposed a severe strain upon the men, but their duties have but increased their ardor, and when the order comes to go to the front the gallant company F will present as fine an appearance as any regiment of regulars. They take pride in these exercises and devote their earnest attention to mastering every detail of a soldier's duty. Captain Rollins, his officers and non-commissioned officers have worked indefatigably to bring their men to a state of perfect efficiency, and the success which has attended their well directed efforts is as pleasing as it is marked. It is safe to assert that the company will acquit themselves on the field in such a manner as to reflect credit not only upon themselves, but also upon the city of Dover to which the majority of them belong. The men have comported themselves in true military style, and although chafing at the delay in taking the field, their conduct has been in every way most exemplary. They are full of patriotism and keep in excellent spirits, the sick list being exceedingly small.

The Sawyer Rifles.

CO. D. FIRST REGIMENT NEW HAMPSHIRE NATIONAL GUARD.

The Sawyer Rifles was organized May 1, 1887, and was named for Hon. Charles H. Sawyer. The officers are; Captain, David Y. Robinson; First Lieutenant, Charles H. Hanson. Their Armory is located in Lowell's Hall, Third street, where regular drills are held. About forty men constitute the company, but during the American-Spanish war it was recruited to its full strength. The officers and men were much chagrined at not being called out for active service, and several volunteered and were accepted as recruits in the Strafford Guards when they received orders to go to the front. The company was detailed as an escort for the Strafford Guards and accompanied them from the armory to the depot when they left Dover for Concord, Saturday, May 7th, 1898.

Dover of To-day.

Dover is eligibly situated on the Cocheco river, surrounded by fertile farms and
located in one of the most beautiful sections of the state. It is in the eastern part
of Strafford county, sixty-one miles from
Concord, and sixty-eight miles from Boston, on the main line of the great Boston
& Maine railroad, being the focal point of
several branches of that system, which
radiate from the city and cover the entire
contiguous territory. Boston can be
reached in two hours, there being numerous passenger trains to and from the city
daily. Dover is bounded on the north by
Rochester and
So m e rsworth,
on the east by
So m e rsworth,
Rollinsford
and the Salmon
Falls river,
which sepa-
rates it from
the State of
Maine, on the
south by Mad-
bury, and the
Piscataqua riv-
er, and on the
west by Mad-
bury and Bar-
rington. The
Cocheco river
r u n s through
the heart of the
city and is navi-
gable to vessels of light draught from the
ocean to the landing, the scenery along its
banks, particularly at Dover Point, being
singularly beautiful. The falls are thirty-one
and one-half feet high and an abundance of
power is furnished to the great mills, much
of which is still available for manufacturing purposes. The Cocheco and Salmon
Falls rivers join some distance below the
city. Dover is the recognized commercial
centre of Strafford county, being the shire
town and the seat of the county government. The census of 1890 gave a population of 12,841, representing 3,000 families, and the present estimated population
is about 14,000. The assessed polls are

STRAFFORD COUNTY COURT HOUSE.

3,122 and the voting strength is 2,700.
The latest assessor's figures give the city a
total valuation of $9,000,000 approxima te-
ly, the tax rate being $1.95 per hundred.

RESIDENTIAL.

If beauty of situation, benefits of unexcelled business opportunity, all that is wise
in conservatism, united with all that is
noble in the grand progressive movement
of the present age ; if surroundings eleva-
ting in influence, institutions helpful in an
honorable struggle with the vicissitudes of
practical life ; if health, wealth and happi-
ness are attractions in a place of residence,
then Dover truly recommends herself as
                                e s s e n t ially a
                                pleasant place to
                                live in. The
                                resident of Do-
                                ver, be he work-
                                man with hands
                                or brain, may
                                have his o w n
                                home, m a d e
                                attainable by the
                                large industries
                                w h i c h readily
                                exchange money
                                for good service,
                                and by low rents
                                with room for
                                the g a r d e n.
                                These combined
                                with the cheap-
                                ness of the over-
                                flowing h o m e
                                market relieve
him from an existence of mere animal
slavery to the common needs of life.
Thus the manufacturer and capitalist
seeking a home in Dover finds his interests
and the safety and well-being of society
resting on a sound, secure basis of well-
conditioned labor. A larger question and
one of greater import than the mere question of labor to the man planting his business here, is that the whole conduct of the
affairs of the city by the selection of its
officers, is in the hands of intelligent
people who make Dover their permanent
home, and do not leave us to the mercy
of a shifting population. Our building
facilities, too, are unexcelled. The best

of building stone, especially for foundations, can be bought at little expense, and good bricks are made from the best of clay within our borders so cheaply that we ship them in large quantities to Boston and other places. The river enables us to bring timber and lime to our wharves at reasonable rates. The superior system of public schools ; the inestimable benefits of the religious privileges afforded by the many church-

various requirements of the types of men and women in whose lives the term and place of home takes a predisposing part. Dover's streets are wide, well kept and lined with beautiful and luxuriant shade trees. There are numerous pleasant residential streets, and the important business thoroughfares are Central avenue, which runs through the heart of the city, Washington and Locust streets. There are two important squares—Central and Franklin.

GOVERNMENT.

The City Government is vested in a Mayor and Board of ten Aldermen, elected annually, two by each ward, and a Common Council, three members being elected annually from each of the five wards. The mayor presides over the board of aldermen, the president of the council being elected each year from among the members. The city hall, a massive and stately building, faces on Central avenue and cost $225,000.

RELIGIOUS.

Religion, the recog-

A GROUP OF DOVER'S CHURCHES.

es ; the advantages of our free public library, and the most charming social circles—all these advantages in location of healthful climate and sanitary local influences, together with the business prospects and opportunities of the city, make it, as it were, a medley of substantial attractions as a residence singularly suited to the

nition of God as an object of worship, love and obedience, the corner-stone on which our civilization rests, must occupy a place in every man's thoughts. The churches of Dover are widely distributed, and are confined to no section. The ecclesiastical edifices are mostly of substantial and enduring proportions and the condition of their financial affairs attests the most skilful and conservative direction. There are thirteen churches: two Congregational, two Free-will Baptist, two Roman Catholic, Friends, Unitarian, Episcopal, Methodist, Second Advent, Calvinist Baptist, and Universalist.

Some of the church edifices are beautiful in architectural design and finish and the pastors are zealous, efficient and im-bued with a sense of their duties and re-sponsibilities. The Christian sentiment of the city is intelligent, earnest, watchful and persistent, and is manifesting an activ-ity that will secure to Dover abundant church privileges, and well planted centres

ing chosen by the City Councils. Their sanitation, heating and ventilation are care-fully attended to, and the course of study prescribed is judiciously selected to meet the requirements necessary for the impart-ing of a sound education to the pupils. The High school is situated on Chestnut street and its curriculum is of the highest order. Its certificate of graduation entitles the holder to step into Dartmouth college without further qualification. There are four Grammar schools: the Sawyer, Bel-knap, Sherman and Pine Hill; five Prim-ary schools, the Sawyer, Peirce, Varney, Hale and Welch; four Ungraded schools, Garrison Hill, Back River, Upper and Lower Neck; and two Pa-rochial schools—those of St Joseph's and the Sacred Heart.

LOCUST STREET AND CENTRAL AVENUE.

of a healthy Christian influence in the years to come. The Y. M. C. A., the Salvation Army and numerous efforts in the line of mission work also receive en-couragement and support.

EDUCATIONAL.

The schools of Dover are regarded with much favor by our citizens and large ap-propriations are devoted to their use each year by the city government. They are under the control and direction of a School Committee consisting of fifteen members, each ward electing one member annually for two years, the remaining members be-

The teaching force numbers forty-five, and the total enrollment of pupils is 1,608, exclusive of the Parochial schools. The rule adopted by the committee October 4, 1897, that " In the election of new teach-ers preference will be given to candidates holding state certificates, or those who are graduates of a normal school or a college, other qualifications being equal," is likely to be far-reaching in its influence, and to exercise a constant tendency towards raising the standard of the teaching force. There is also a well managed and largely attended business college, where pupils are fitted for commercial pursuits.

FRANKLIN SQUARE.

While reasonable conservatism has characterized the management of Dover's banking institutions—it is not to be presumed that they are by any means lacking in enterprise or that safe and careful kind of public spirit that stands ready to extend proper assistance to public and private movements based on correct principles for development of resources, the prosecution of improvements, the upholding of legitimate business ventures and the establishment and assistance of manufactures and commerce. On the contrary, as will readily be attested on all hands, these institutions have frequently acted with liberality and promptitude in cases of public and private need and thus earned the respect and confidence of the general community. The officers and directors of these banks are men of broad views, large capital and capacity identified with the city's best interests and prepared at all times to contribute of their time, labor and means for her material advancement. The banks comprise two National and two Savings banks with a combined capital and deposits of over $7,000,000 and a co-operative bank founded in 1890 and since most successfully operated. The large insurance companies, both home and foreign, have representatives here and a substantial and ever increasing business is carried on.

SCENE ON THE ROAD TO DOVER POINT.

Boston & Maine connecting the city with the markets of the north, east, south and west and the Cocheco river, navigable from the ocean to the landing, material necessarily accumulates here and cheap power and abundant skilled labor are amply provided and assured for all time. Opportunities can be had here by the manufacturer superior to those of larger cities, for the reason that while equal facilities are found here, at the same time the best and most central positions are available at comparatively little cost, and numerous sites on the lines of railroad and on the river banks are open for use. The manufacturer who locates here will find everything at hand for the successful furtherance of his enterprise, and a friendly and helping hand will be offered to him by our citizens.

No city in the world offers more advantages to the small or large manufacturer than Dover. The introduction of new enterprises will increase the opportunities for the retail merchant to establish successful mercantile operations. The question has frequently been asked, what can be manufactured in Dover to the best advantage? The simplest answer and an absolutely true one is *everything*. The textile interests are very extensive and have been the chief factor in the upbuilding of the city. Half a dozen boot and shoe factories are at present operated here ; a machine shop, manufacturing stoves, ranges and large machinery ; one of the largest belting concerns in the country ; wood working machinery shops ; twelve large brick yards, located on each side of the river ; two carriage factories ; and numerous other industries are successfully carried on and afford constant employment to thousands at remunerative wages.

MANUFACTURING.

The right place to successfully manufacture is evidently at a point where the raw material accumulates naturally, and where, at the same time, there are cheap power and advanced and ample facilities for marketing the product. Dover has for many years furnished these conditions. With the great railroad system of the

The city escaped to a marked degree the recent extended commercial depression, and throughout the relations of employer and employee have been amicable and no strikes have paralyzed our great textile industries or caused a moment's anxiety to their proprietors.

RETAIL BUSINESS.

Capital and business enterprises have given Dover good stores, wholesale and retail, the stocks of merchandise and other essentials being rich and varied, and, as freight rates are comparatively low, prices

cess, and so long as the commercial interests of Dover are in the hands of such men as its present merchants, a still larger measure of prosperity is assured beyond a peradventure of doubt.

TRANSPORTATION AND COMMUNICATION.

The transportation facilities of Dover are largely in the hands of the Boston and Maine and the Union Electric railway companies. The Western Union and Postal companies furnish telegraphic and cable service to all the world. The New England Telephone and Telegraph company

CUSHING STREET.

are quoted accordingly, so that people from the surrounding districts come here to buy, while the wholesale trade, especially in the leading staples, serves the surrounding sections. The business men are so fully alive and attentive to the wants of the community that there is no necessity for going outside to get anything, for here everything that can be required by a family can be had of the latest pattern or fashion, and at prices which compare favorably with those ruling in the great metropolitan centres. These enterprises are managed with considerable energy and suc-

maintains communication with the surrounding towns, and their long distance service enables patrons to converse with people in all the large cities of America with ease. The American, Jackson and Dover and Boston expresses, with a large number of local carriers do a general transportation business.

PUBLIC IMPROVEMENTS.

Gas and electricity are extensively used by the citizens of Dover for lighting purposes, being abundantly supplied by the United Gas and Electric Company. Electricity is exclusively used for street lighting, the arc lamps numbering 130, and are placed so as to afford the best possible results and effectively lighting every part of the city. Among the most valuable and necessary of our recent public improvements has been the installation of a perfect system of water-works at an outlay of over $355,000, which are now self-supporting. The water-takers number 1,745, and are supplied daily with an average of 600,000 gallons. The pumping station, with a capacity of pumping 2,000,-000 gallons a day is located near Garrison Hill. The supply is drawn from Willand's Pond which is augmented by springs and artesian wells. The

red brick structure, ranking relatively as one of the finest public buildings in New England. The streets and highways are improved materially each year, the appropriations and additions last year being: highways, $17,236.75 ; sidewalks, $2,000 ; sewers, $3,650 ; street paving, $2,573.98. These sums have been expended judiciously and with most gratifying results to our residents. A park commission of three members care for the city park at Garrison Hill, which forms a pleasant retreat during the summer months. Central park,

VIEWS ON CENTRAL AVENUE.

reservoir is on the summit of Garrison Hill. The system has thirty miles of mains, and sixteen miles of service piping. The city hall, formally dedicated in 1891, contains a beautifully decorated and excellently equipped opera house, capable of seating 1,800 people ; public library containing 22,714 volumes of the choicest literature ; armory ; police station and court room, with ample office accommodation for the city officials. The building was erected at a cost of $225,000, and is a stately

situated on the line of the Union Electric railway, and containing twenty acres tastefully laid out as pleasure grounds is much frequented, good boating being obtainable at Willand's Pond. In the course of nature, resting places for the dead must be set apart. Pine Hill Cemetery was granted to the city for burial purposes, March 29, 1731, and is at present under the careful management and solicitous care of a board of five trustees, one of whose members is elected annually by the board of trustees and board of aldermen in convention, the mayor being a member ex-officio. The other cemeteries are St. Mary's old cemetery, on Stark avenue, and the new cemetery of St. Mary's on the Dover Point road.

HISTORICAL, LITERARY AND SOCIAL INSTITUTIONS, ETC.

Among the most prominent of these may be mentioned the Dover Historical Society, the Public Library, the Young Men's Catholic Literary Society and the Bellamy Club. In the matter of secret, benevolent, fraternal and social societies the various degrees of Masonry, Odd Fellowship, Knights of Pythias, Elks, Red Men and others are liberally represented, and have a large membership. There are several social clubs, and numerous musical, labor, legal, fraternal, press, medical, temperance, political, military and school organizations, Y. M. C. A., G. A. R., Sons of Veterans, Women's Relief Corps, etc.

THE MASONIC TEMPLE.

CHARITABLE INSTITUTIONS.

The buildings of the Wentworth home for the aged have recently been completed at a cost of $15,000. The home is named for Hon. Arioch Wentworth, of Boston, whose birthplace is in the immediate vicinity, and who generously donated $10,000 for its erection and equipment and subsequently gave $20,000 towards a permanent fund. It contains twenty-three sleeping apartments, and seven other rooms used as parlors, dining-room, pantry and matron's room. The Hayes hospital, for the endowment of which Mrs. Clara A.

L. McD. Hayes left $50,000 will shortly be in operation. The Children's home recently completed at an expenditure of $15,000 will accommodate forty homeless orphans and destitute children. There is also the Orphan's home under the control of St. Mary's parish church and in charge of the Sisters of mercy. For those less fortunate than their fellows the county farm provides accommodation at the city's expense, and is also used as a reformatory.

POLICE.

The police force of the city is under the control of the Mayor and City Councils and is under the direction of a marshal and assistant marshal. The patrol consists of two day, and six night men, placed in the business and residential sections to the best advantage. Although the tenure of the entire force is upon an annual basis, changes are rarely made, the services of most of the officers and the patrol extending over a period of years. The able and unbiased work for which the force is noted has its reward in continued incumbency of office.

FIRE DEPARTMENT.

The fire department is thoroughly efficient, and reflects much credit upon the city. It is under the control of the city councils, who elect a chief engineer and two assistants. There are three hose companies, a hook and ladder company, and the hydrant service is augmented by three steamers, one of which is always in

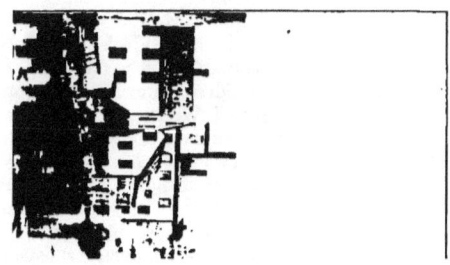

commission. There are also three hose wagons, one hose reel, one supply wagon, and one hand engine which is located at the city farm. The city is covered with the fire alarm telegraph system, twenty-nine alarm boxes, three tower strikers and one steam gong being placed at convenient points throughout the city. There are thirteen hydrants for steamers, and twenty-six reservoirs and the water supply is adequate to any demand made upon it, ranging from 60 to 125 pounds pressure.

THE DOVER PUBLIC LIBRARY.

Back in the days before the Declaration of Independence, when New Hampshire was still an English colony, there existed in Dover a Social Library which numbered among its membership the best citizens of the town. This Library was incorporated in 1792, the only year that the Legislature ever convened at Dover, and was the first incorporated Social Library in the State. It was the predecessor, if not the ancestor, of the circulating libraries which later served the reading needs of the people and of the corporate body known as the Dover Library, which was formed in 1850.

As early as 1856,—the Boston Public Library was founded only six years earlier,—the suggestion was made in the librarian's annual report, E. J. Lane being then librarian, that the library should be made public and " worthy of the city." Similar suggestions followed as years went on and public sentiment in favor of the change increased until January, 1883, when in his inaugural address as mayor of the city, Dr. James E. Lothrop brought the matter actively before the city government. Action was at once taken. A contract was made by the city, with the Dover Library, under the terms of which the city agreed to provide for the necessary expenses of the Library perpetually, and the Dover Library turned over to the city about 5000 volumes and $2432.10 in cash. The money was the principal and interest of a bequest made by Mr. William N. Andrews, a merchant of this city, who had hoped that the gift might aid in the establishment of a Public Library. The legacy was placed in the hands of Mr. James W.

Bartlett as trustee and kept for the purpose the giver desired.

The Board of Trustees of the Dover Public Library as first organized was as follows :—James E. Lothrop, Mayor, Trustee ex-officio. John C. Pray, President of the Common Council, Trustee ex-officio. Jeremiah Smith, Joshua G. Hall, Z. S. Wallingford, T. B. Garland from the Dover Library. Joshua L. Foster, John T. Welch, Martin S. Hutchings from the city. President, James E. Lothrop ; Secretary, John T. Welch ; Treasurer, Frank Freeman.

The first librarian was Mr. T. B. Garland who after five months service resigned, and his daughter, the present librarian, until then acting as assistant, was appointed. Miss Beatrice M. Jenkins, who had been temporary assistant was made first assistant, a position which she still holds. In 1887 the growth of the Library demanded a second assistant, and Miss Stella Smith received the appointment. She was succeeded by Miss Alice O. Folsom, and in September, 1889, Miss Ida F. Hollingworth, the present cataloguer, took the place. A third assistant has now become necessary and Miss Bessie I. Parker has been promoted from temporary to permanent assistant.

The story of the Library is a story of steady growth. When it opened to the public in January, 1884, it contained about 5000 volumes. It has now 23,000 volumes. During its first year 50,200 books were loaned for home use, a number then far in excess of any other library in the State. Last year 73,500 books were given out, and the proportion of fiction and juvenile reading had decreased from 78 to 65 per cent. Systematic co-operation is kept up between the public schools and the library, and in many schools pupils are now trained to an intelligent use of books as part of their education.

The Library has always been dependent upon the city for its maintenance and each year the City Councils reckon it in among the necessary expenses and give to it as large a sum as possible. In 1888 a bequest of one thousand dollars came to it by the will of Dr. T. J. W. Pray and in 1896, one of two thousand by the will of Mrs. Elizabeth Hale Jaques. Nearly four hundred volumes of the Law Library were the gift of the estate of Frank Hobbs.

The Historical room contains the local history that the Library has been collecting, comprising files of early newspapers, nearly all the town histories of the State, the Provincial Papers and many works of great historical and genealogical value. The Reading Room has on its tables about a hundred periodicals and papers and together with the Reference Library and the Law Library is open to all.

The Board of Trustees have always been men of high standing in the community. They have made as few restrictions as possible in the use of the Library, deeming it for the best interests of the city that a policy of wide freedom should prevail. Free access to books, excellent catalogue facilities, and willing service are the principles upon which the Library has been conducted, and which will insure its usefulness in the future.

DOVER COMMERCIAL CLUB.

The Dover Commercial Club was organized in 1896, with a membership of 125, its first president being Colonel A. T. Peirce. It is a body of representative citizens who will gladly communicate with those having unemployed capital and who are interested in the establishment of manufactories, and will aid all new enterprises of sterling worth that will advance Dover's commercial prestige, increase her population and benefit the community. Seldom, if ever, has such an earnest desire been expressed to direct capital and manufacturing industries here as at present. The objects of the Commercial Club are to inculcate just and equitable principles in trade ; to acquire, preserve and disseminate valuable business information ; to protect and foster the mercantile and manufacturing industries ; to promote the commerce of Dover and its general prosperity by the solicitation of manufacturing and business enterprises to locate within its boundaries ; the continuous promulgation of the advantages possessed by Dover as a desirable place for the employment of capital ; the extension of facilities for transportation and the protection of the trade of the city. They have actively and

practically encouraged the location of manufacturing enterprises of all kinds by offering to have exempted from taxation for a period of five years all manufacturing industries locating here. All that is essential is that those who avail themselves of these inducements be men possessing thorough practical and technical knowledge of the business they propose to undertake. The present officers of the Commercial Club are :—President, Thomas H. Dearborn ; Directors, Jas. E. Lothrop, Valentine Mathes, A. C. Place, Henry Law, J. Frank Seavey, Frank N. French and George E. Buzzell ; Secretary, George D. Barrett.

DOVER NAVIGATION CO.

The Dover Navigation Company was organized in 1878, with a capital stock of $13,121.92 which was increased from time to time until in 1889 it reached the sum of $212,626.73. The company was formed for the purpose of building vessels and engaging in the coasting trade, and their ships have since been carrying cargoes between ports on the Atlantic seaboard, the Gulf of Mexico, the West Indies and South America. The original board of management consisted of Colonel John Bracewell, President, C. H. Trickey, Thomas B. Garland, J. Frank Seavey and B. Frank Nealley. A new vessel was built each year until the company owned ten. Of these three were sold, two lost and five are still engaged in the coastwise carrying trade, carrying mostly lumber and coal. The capital stock of the company is at present $104,522.21, and between July 1878 and July 1898, $238,110.66 has been returned to the stockholders in dividends. Of the original capital, $62,600 has been returned. The company has done much to promote and stimulate the commerce of the city which has derived decided advantages from the success of the undertaking.

DOVER IMPROVEMENT ASSOCIATION.

The object of this institution, in brief, is the promotion of the welfare and prosperity of the city by bringing to it valuable industries which can not fail to be of inestimable value in building up its commercial supremacy. Through its labors two large shoe shops have been added to the manufactories already in operation. The pay rolls of these companies alone amount to several thousand dollars a month, and employment is given to a large number of persons, thus adding considerably to the prosperity and well-being of the city. The Association had its inception in 1885, when it was organized with a capital of $50,000. Hon. J. E. Lothrop is president and Thomas B. Garland Secretary and Treasurer. In 1885 the Association built the large five story brick factory measuring 200x45, now occupied by J. H. Ireland & Co. of Newburyport, Mass., who hold it rent free for a term of

circumstances to arrest its growth, either as a place of business or residence. The past of Dover having furnished a record of continuous and sustained growth it is a fair presumption that the future will present results of proportionate advance or even accelerated expansion. In the utilization of all the resources which nature has furnished or science unveiled, there is every reason to believe that Dover will be fully abreast with the most progressive cities. It has no lack of men with business sagacity equal to the improvement of every opportunity, and it is safe to predict that the industries of the future will be able to point back to those of today as the auspicious beginnings of a greater

STRAFFORD COUNTY JAIL.

ten years. The second factory was built in 1894, and is a four story wooden structure measuring 150x45, now occupied by Charles E. Moulton, shoe manufacturer, at a very low rental. The establishment of this Association is an instance of the progressive and enterprising spirit which prevails among our citizens, who are ever on the alert to materially advance the city's best interests and offer inducements of a substantial nature to manufacturers and capitalists to locate their business in Dover.

PROSPECTS FOR THE FUTURE.

The location of Dover is one which renders it impossible for any combination of

and brighter destiny. The present of Dover is magnificent and full of promise. Its natural advantages were never better supplemented by its acquired resources for the development of its progress than they are today. It is the home of intellectual vigor, wealth, manufactures and commerce, with a past full of interest, a present full of earnestness and a future full of brightness and continued prosperity.

Wentworth Home for the Aged.

The Wentworth Home for the Aged, that new and beautiful edifice, a most modern structure situated in the northern extremity of Central avenue, was dedicated on Saturday afternoon, June 25th, 1898, with due ceremony and exercises befitting the occasion. It will stand as a monument for generations to come to the memory of that distinguished philanthropist, Mr. Arioch Wentworth of Boston, whose munificent gift it was. The citizens of Dover may well feel proud of such a worthy institution, second to none of its kind in the State where her citizens when homeless and helpless, with the infirmities of old age creeping upon them, will have as their home a place where they can rest assured they will be well cared for. Located as it is upon a healthful elevation, a spot where no better atmosphere can be desired, looking down from its majestic height and in its absolute quietness upon the busy city with surroundings most delightful to the eye, it is safe to say that a more appropriate site could not have been selected. Landscape gardeners through the generosity of Hon. Frank Jones have, with skilled hands beautified the grounds and added much to their general appearance. The Home in itself is a modest yet imposing structure every room of which is now elaborately furnished and ready for inmates.

The building is a three-story brick structure with granite trimmings, and resembles somewhat the colonial mansion so common in this part of New England.

ARIOCH WENTWORTH.

The architect, Alvah T. Ramsdell of this city, designed the building with special reference to insuring the ease and comfort of aged people. The building is 70 by 53 feet in dimension and contains 30 rooms, besides toilet and bathrooms. A hallway extends through the entire length of the building and opens on to broad, sunny verandas at either end and in front.

On the left of the main entrance is the matron's room and library. This is furnished by Miss Caroline Wendell. On the right are the reception and sitting rooms, furnished respectively by the daughters of the late Hon. Wm. S. Stevens and Mrs. Judge Durell. On the further side of the hall are the dining room and kitchen, each 16x12 feet, and pantry.

There are three sleeping rooms on the first floor, and 11 each on the second and third floors. The furnishings of the sleeping rooms are all of the same pattern though of different shades of carpets and upholstering. They were all furnished by residents as memorials to departed relatives. The building is finished in oak and sycamore and the walls are tinted in warm colors. In the hall is an old fashioned tall clock, presented by C. W. Demeritt, and a piano, the gift of Mrs. J. E. Lothrop.

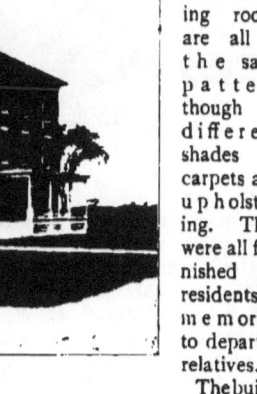

WENTWORTH HOME.

Col. Daniel Hall in his introductory address outlined the history of the movement for establishing a home for aged people in this city. He said in part, that through the efforts of Col. Everett O. Foss an act was passed by the legislature of 1883 incorporating "The Dover Home for Aged Women." The first contribution was made on Christmas day, 1885, when 14 members of the Bachelor club gave $1 each as a Christmas offer to start a fund. Since then gifts have been made by individuals and societies, and one or two bequests. In 1897 a gift of $10,000 was made by Mr. Wentworth for the purpose of building a suitable home, and in recognition of this generous aid the association voted to name the building in honor of the donor, calling it the "Wentworth Home for the Aged."

Before concluding his address Col. Hall announced that the association has just received from Mr. Wentworth another gift of $20,000 to be used as a fund for the support of the home.

CHILDREN'S HOME.

The news was received with the greatest enthusiasm.

The contributions to a Permanent Fund are as follows : Mr. Arioch Wentworth, Boston, $20,000 ; Mrs. S. E. W. Creighton, Newmarket, $1,000 ; Mrs. Elizabeth W. Stevens, Boston, $500 ; Mrs. Sarah E. Drew, Dover, $500 ; Miss Martha E. Hanson, Dover, $500 : Mrs. Deborah Dunn, Dover, $100.

Mr. Arioch Wentworth was born in Rollinsford, just over the Dover line, his birthplace being less than a mile from where the new home is situated.

The officers of the association in charge of the home are : Joseph B. Sawyer, pres. ;

Harrison Haley and Thomas B. Garland, vice pres. ; Charles S. Cartland, sec. and treas. : Daniel Hall, auditor.

There is a board of twenty trustees of which Elisha R. Brown is chairman, an executive committee of one hundred members and a board of managers.

The Children's Home.

Few fathers and mothers situated in beautiful and commodious homes with their children playing about their knees think of the many little waifs in this city who know nothing of the pleasures of even the most meagre home. For their benefit and in their honor the beautiful building on Locust street was constructed and the citizens of this city realize the grand work that the managers of the Children's Home have been doing for the past few years. The edifice is beautiful in both exterior and interior, arranged in accordance with the best sanitary models, commodious in room and handsomely finished. The Home contains dining and reception rooms, nursery, boys' and girls' dormitory, matron's room and boys' and girls' play rooms, bath rooms, and several large sleeping rooms. On the third floor a room has been finished so that in case of any contagious disease breaking out among the children it can be closed up and the patient kept from the other children. This room has been nicely fitted up for sickness and has a bath room and many other conveniences.

Several of the rooms at the Home have been furnished by the following persons :

Reception room, Mrs. John P. Hale; assembly room, Mrs. John S. Glass; dining room, Miss Caroline Wendell. The nursery room has been furnished by the Mizpah club of the First church. Many other articles have been donated by generous persons for the other rooms.

In the basement of the building is a large store room and place for the coal. At the rear is a well arranged laundry with set of boilers and laundry heaters. The building is heated by steam, there being a radiator in every room. A. T. Ramsdell was the architect who designed the building, the corner stone of which was laid on Saturday, Oct. 9, 1897, with appropriate ceremonies. The contract was given to E. H. Frost on Aug. 30, 1897, for $9,849. He has done an excellent piece of work on

sponded in accepting the keys. There was then reading of the Scripture by Rev. E. A. Hoyt, pastor of the Pierce Memorial church, and singing. Rev. I. W. Beard then formally dedicated the building using the Episcopal service provided for such occasions. Prayer was offered by Rev. George E. Hall, D. D., followed by singing by the children of the home.

Appropriate remarks were then made by Rev. D. C. Babcock and Rev. R. E. Gilkey, and the service closed by singing the Doxology.

Among the gifts to the Children's Home have been $5,000 from Mr. Arioch Wentworth of Boston, $5,000 from W. H. Morton, wife and daughter of Salmon Falls, $500 from Mrs. David L. Drew of

CENTRAL SQUARE.

the structure. The building committee who have had charge of the work have attended to their duties faithfully and are deserving of much praise. The committee is as follows: W. S. Bradley, J. Herbert Richardson, Hon. James E. Lothrop, Mrs. Susan E. Young, Mrs. Lydia E. Jones, Mrs. Ellen F. Carter and Mrs. Elizabeth G. Williams. The dedication occurred Saturday afternoon, May 28, 1898, and the exercises were very appropriate, being of a religious character.

At four o'clock the exercises opened with invocation by Rev. W. H. S. Hascall. The keys of the house were then delivered to the president of the society by W. S. Bradley, the chairman of the building committee, in a few appropriate remarks. The president, Mrs. Susan E. Young, re-

Dover, and numerous lesser gifts from persons interested in the institution. The home is now in complete working order, about thirty children being cared for and trained to careers of usefulness. The benefits of such an institution as this in the community cannot be over-estimated and it is safe to assert that the children who spend their early lives in the Home will acquire habits of thrift and honesty which cannot fail to exercise a most salutary effect upon their future lives.

The urgent need of such an institution as this has long been felt in the city and the carrying out of the project to erect and maintain the Children's Home is one which reflects the greatest credit upon our citizens who have so liberally contributed towards this humanitarian work.

VIEW OF DOVER FROM PINE HILL.

Foster's Daily Democrat.

GEO. J. FOSTER & CO., Proprietors.

DOVER, N. H., JUNE 18, 1898.

Twenty-five years ago to-day, the first issue of Foster's Daily Democrat appeared in Dover. It was a small four page sheet 22x25, a tiny beginner with a somewhat dubious future before it, but plucky and courageous, defiant and confident in the face of all obstacles and determined to succeed. It started with 140 subscribers and 150 copies were sold to those who chose to buy them,— 290 copies comprised the total circulation. But the editor, Joshua L. Foster was not without newspaper experience and he thought he could see ahead clearly enough a much better condition not a great way in the distance, and the result has been no disappointment. The editor's salutation to the public in the first issue June 18, 1873, was as follows :

" We have very little to say in venturing this daily experiment in Dover. It is a new thing here, but not a new business with us who take the risk and the responsibility. It is an experiment which may or may not prove a success, as this depends upon the energy and ability manifested in its conduct, and the alacrity and persistency with which the people come up to its support. We shall strive to fulfill our part, and expect the public to sustain our efforts with their patronage. Dover is the only city in New Hampshire that has hitherto had no daily paper. Concord, Nashua and Portsmouth each have about the same population as this city, and each supports two daily papers. It is certain that Dover and its immediate vicinity ought to support one. There is nothing that can give so much life, pleasure and real, substantial good character to a place as a lively and well conducted daily newspaper. We shall devote these columns mainly to the material and vital interests of Dover and vicinity. Whatever may tend to benefit this people and enhance their prosperity, will receive our warm and enthusiastic support. This paper starts with very flattering prospects, and if we receive the continued encouragement which ought to be given to a properly conducted enterprise of the kind, we shall make this daily an enduring institution in Dover. It is for the people to say how this shall be. Our weekly is a success. Shall this be the same ? "

The experience of the paper the editor gives as follows :—" Flattering prospects " indeed ! Everybody laughed and hooted at the idea, while pretty nearly

JOSHUA L. FOSTER, EDITOR.

A CORNER IN THE EDITORIAL ROOM.

A SECTION OF THE BUSINESS OFFICE.

everybody hoped for the success of the venture, although they didn't believe it would live over three months. The experiment had been tried two or three times before and failed. We said it was because the experimenters didn't know their business. Our faith was a good deal like the grain of mustard seed we had read about, although rather faint at times. Flattering prospects! O yes, very flattering—140 subscribers, half of whom had not paid a cent, and 150 more sold for which we got a cent and a half apiece—$2.25 ready cash from those sales. It was a big thing, a very big thing, with wonderfully " flattering prospects" ahead. We had a little advertising at prices so small as to be hardly seen with the naked eye. The editor was alone in his calculations and management. He had no financial resources, having lost all in a previous venture. He had friends, some of whom helped a little and others not a cent. He had two sons, George J. and Charles G., neither of them old enough to do the business, but both had learned to set up type and were very effective help in that way. Notwithstanding the alleged " flattering prospects " it was up hill work. We had to hire help, buy paper, pay rents, support a family and all that.

GEO. J. FOSTER, BUSINESS MANAGER.

The weekly paper started a year and a half before was doing tolerably well, although we had to trust nearly everybody, get the pay when we could, and lots of it we never got at all. Things went on however, gaining gradually on the whole, barely perceptible, but still slightly moving ahead, hardly keeping square, but doing the best we could. The circulation improved slowly, kept on growing a little larger, and we kept on pegging away. We sent out canvassers and they brought in a few ducats, but we had awful hard work for many years ; sometimes extremely blue, because the help must be paid, the paper bills must be met, and we didn't know how, nor where to get the money. Although a democrat in those days, we had a conscience and were disposed to show it some respect. Of course this being the case, we disagreed with the party leaders in some things and there was a rupture which at the time boded no good to us. Still we spoke our mind freely, just as though we didn't care a pin, and told lots of homely truths about the men who tried to put a ring in our nose and run our thinking as well as printing apparatus. They imported a lurid warrior, bristling with flaming daggers who started another paper to destroy us, but new friends rallied around us,

COMPOSING ROOM.

PRESS ROOM, SHOWING GOSS WEB PERFECTING PRESS.

more practical and less selfish than those we had before, and we "went for" the false ones red hot which they soon found out. Instead of going down, we took the road up, and up we went. When that fight was over and we had gathered up, laid out and buried the dead, we had more friends and a little more money than before. But still we were in the financial swamp and had a struggle to keep head above ground. And there we waded and paddled on until the presidential year 1880 came along and some of the then opposing political brethren started a competing daily, the Republican, to divide with us the enormous profits we were gathering in. It was only for the campaign, but when that was over it changed hands and they concluded to keep it running. And from this point dates the turn of the tide with the DAILY DEMOCRAT.

older one George J., while the younger, Charles G., took charge of and superintended the departments of the interior. The paper had once been enlarged and it was then enlarged again. They went to business as the editor had never been able to do, because editorial and business duties could not all be properly attended to by one man. The editor can write the English language with reasonable accuracy, run a tilt with an adversary in sufficiently effective fashion and make himself understood by the common run of intelligent mankind, but in financial and general executive management, the two sons take the lead. The younger of them has for the past two years acted the important part of assistant editor and done good work in that capacity.

As we have said, from the establishment of a competing paper and the turning over of the business management to

CHARLES G. FOSTER, ASSOCIATE EDITOR.

Meanwhile, during those weary years of anxiety and toil, for nothing but a bare living without a dollar ahead for a rainy day, the two sons had been getting along to maturer years and had learned to do the business. They too had been schooled and had profited by it. A year or two later all the financial and business affairs of the concern were turned over to the the sons of the editor, the paper took on new life and soon bounded to the front. The nominal competition put us all "more on our muscle," as such things generally do, and the circulation and advertising showed it at once. The editorial department, the news department and the business department were all better managed and run, and have been ever since as our success fully proves. Soon after

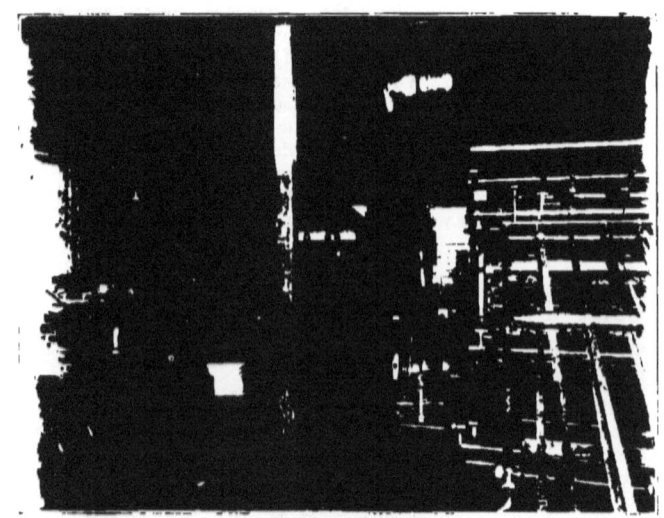

CYLINDER PRESS ROOM.

JOB PRESS ROOM.

these things happened, the democratic party in 1885 succeeded to the executive power in the nation, but with no honor to itself or the country. So false and un-American was its policy, so cowardly and perfidious were its leaders that the continuance of our adhesion and support involved the loss of the confidence of the better portions of the community, and, of more importance still, if possible, the sacrifice of our self respect. As was our clearest right, we took our own course, and the public support we have since received is the best evidence that we made no mistake.

The DAILY DEMOCRAT is the pioneer of local newspaper work in the State. The first to adopt and make c o n s p i c u o u s the purely local feature in that work, employing special local reporters to gather in all home transactions worthy of note, thus securing and holding the local attention and support, it has lived to see all others follow its example and adopt this feature which they n e v e r thought of before, and it really gives the most important and essential value to the local journals everywhere. Also the first to bring into the state the telegraphic news service of the American Press Association, it has seen all others follow on until that too covers the entire field. To this we have also added the very latest Associated Press service which has become the very conspicuous feature of our daily editions, furnishing, as it does, the latest telegraphic news possible for our people to obtain and read at their homes each night when the labors of the day are closed. So now, being the most profitable and best newspaper property, with one of the best office plants in the state,

FRANK P. WALDRON, CITY EDITOR.

on we go. There is no such word as fail or halt in this concern. Nothing but the best will ever satisfy us and that we shall have, cost what it may.

From a very small beginning as we have related, with second hand printing material, presses and type badly worn, purchased on credit and paid for in installments, as best we could, and the one man sinews as the power to turn the wheel about 400 an hour, sweating, panting and foaming as he applied his muscle at the crank; from this delightful state of things we have gone on to what is seen today. Five times has the paper been enlarged and four times have new presses and additional s t e a m power been purchased to do our newspaper printing until we now have one of the latest improved, fast running web perfecting stereotype presses, capable of turning out 10,000 copies per hour of perfect papers printed on both sides from stereotype plates, c u t, folded a n d counted all at once. And the paper h a s grown in size and circulation until it is now an eight page seven columns to the page sheet, 35x47, w i t h supplements when necessary, having a daily circulation of from 3500 to 7000, depending on the character of the news and the height of public excitement; on some occasions it goes as high as 10,000 copies. The circulation reaches out into all the neighboring towns and cities in New Hampshire and Maine, to a constituency of some 60,000 people. It goes into a large majority of the families in a circuit of 25 miles, principally to the north, east and west of the office of publication, and has come to be the chief reliance for local, city and county news. The circulation is constantly increasing,

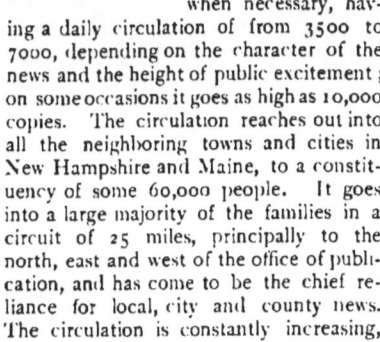

notably since the war with Spain has been the chief topic of public interest. From steam we have changed to electric power, and it requires a 20 H. P. motor to drive our machinery. There are constantly employed in the office 18 persons, and also connected with the paper are eight reporters and correspondents, and more when occasion requires. New type has been several times provided and job presses added until we have as well equipped a printing office as any necessity requires. A poor beggarly concern has grown to be as robust and stalwart an institution of the kind as there is in the state or anywhere northerly or easterly of Boston.

It has all come from hard work and earnest persistent purpose to meet the public desires, to reach the popular heart, to serve the people, to build up Dover and its near community, and always champion what seemed to be the best interests of the whole. Now here we are this 25th anniversary day. No previous day of our life ever saw the DAILY DEMOCRAT in so good, sound, healthy and growing condition, as it is today. Owning this and other resources free from the incubus of debt, it is booming as never before, and is a constant reminder of the rapid and important progress which a quarter century can accomplish in these hurrying times. Dover has grown and everything has grown almost beyond comprehension. This country is the greatest and best on the globe. We have liberties and privileges such as nobody on the earth ever enjoyed or saw before. A happy nation, state and city, all are ours. A happy people indeed. The sun never shone on the like before, and God help us all to pre-

PATRICK MONE, SOMERSWORTH REPORTER.

serve and maintain it as the most precious of all that is possible to enjoy in this world.

We append hereto a sketch prepared by the late Dr. A. H. Quint for the History of Rockingham and Strafford counties recently published :—

"Foster's Democrat," a weekly newspaper, was established in the city of Dover, N. H., in January, 1872, by George J. Foster & Co., and has been issued on Friday of each week ever since. On the 18th of June, 1873, the same firm issued the first number of Foster's Daily Democrat. On these journals J. L. Foster is the editor, and his two sons, George J. and Charles G., are the business managers. The daily venture was made as an experiment, the success of which was at that time generally considered to be very doubtful. But the proprietors decided to push it at all hazards. They thought they knew their business, and the result has proved that they were not mistaken. Several previous attempts had been made by other parties to establish and sustain a daily newspaper in Dover, but they had always failed for lack of experience and business capacity of the projectors. But the senior Foster in this case had seen a good many years of editorial experience, while the juniors were practical printers and trained in the business management of a daily newspaper. In these weekly and daily enterprises the proprietors started out full of pluck and energy, determined, as they said, to make things lively, and treat everybody and all subjects fairly, squarely, and honestly, giving all sides in all cases a chance to be heard, and granting all shades of honest opinion a medium of expression before the public.

These journals are boldly *independent*, running with no mere machine as such, the organs of no ring, wearing nobody's collar, and while ready to listen to all good advice, will submit to no dictation in regard to their conduct or management from any source whatever. They have a large and increasing circulation, their advertising support is liberal and generous, and alike profitable to publishers and patrons. The Senior Foster, assisted by such local and other reporters as may be necessary, devotes his whole time and attention to the editorial conduct of the papers, while the two sons have entire

They have an extensive reading and influence in the community. Starting with very meagre means, the concern has grown to yield a handsome income, and is a very valuable property as well as an important journalistic enterprise of the city and state."

Such words of praise and commendation coming wholly unsolicited from a man such as the Revd. Dr. Quint, whose reputation as a literateur was far reaching, is an eloquent tribute to the merits of the paper not only as a means of disseminating news but also of inculcating those principles of equity and justice upon which

RESIDENCE OF CHARLES G. FOSTER, WEST CONCORD STREET.

charge of the printing and business departments, employing the competent subordinates necessary to meet all requirements.

Connected with these newspapers is a large and well-appointed job printing office, with good workmen constantly employed. The whole establishment is provided with the best modern machinery, driven by electric power, and its several departments are continuously engaged in thrifty and profitable business. The success of these newspapers proves that they are well conducted and enterprising.

the well-being of the community at large rest.

The high standard upon which the foundation of Foster's Daily Democrat was built has been rigidly adhered to and will be always maintained. It has from its inception aimed to be a journal of the highest grade, giving the news of the world, but sedulously avoiding the sensational and salacious now such a common feature of papers less careful of their utterances. A brilliant and prosperous past and present predicts a splendid future for the paper.

RESIDENCE OF JOSHUA L. FOSTER, HANSON STREET.

RESIDENCE OF GEORGE J. FOSTER, HOUGH AND MOUNT VERNON STREETS.

The Cocheco Manufacturing Co.

There is no single interest in the city of Dover that will at once so completely represent the solid character of the city's commercial growth and indicate the quality of its citizenship than what is to be found under the roofs of the Cocheco Manufacturing Company.

In 1810, two years before the establishment of the cotton industry in Dover, the population numbered but 2,228. The embargo and the war of 1812 interfering

nearly doubled, the census of 1830 showing it to be 5,449 ; that of 1840, 6,458 ; of 1850, 8,168 ; and of 1860, 8,502. The increase has been steadily maintained owing largely to the steady and remunerative employment to be found in the factories.

The Dover Cotton Factory was incorporated December 15, 1812, with a capital of $50,000, which built in 1815 the No. 1 factory at Upper Factory Village ; it was a wooden structure and has long since disappeared. The company had its capital enlarged June 21, 1821 to $500,000,

COCHECO MFG. CO.'S DAM.

with mercantile pursuits, the business men of the town embarked in other industries. In that year the Dover Cotton Factory was incorporated. and as the lower falls were supposed to be fully occupied by other mills, the first factory was built two miles up the river and was long known as the upper factory.

The rapid advancement of the town in wealth and population dates from the establishment of this great enterprise. In 1820 the population was 2,870. Within the next ten years these numbers had

about the time when it bought up the titles of the Lower Falls. The capital was enlarged June 17, 1823 to $1,000,000 and the name changed to the Dover Manufacturing Company, but it was not successful and a new company, the present Cocheco Manufacturing Company, was incorporated June 27, 1827, with a capital of $1,000,000, which purchased of the old company all their works and property.

No. 2 mill was built in 1822 but this building ceased to be called No. 2 when the new No. 2 (first section), on the

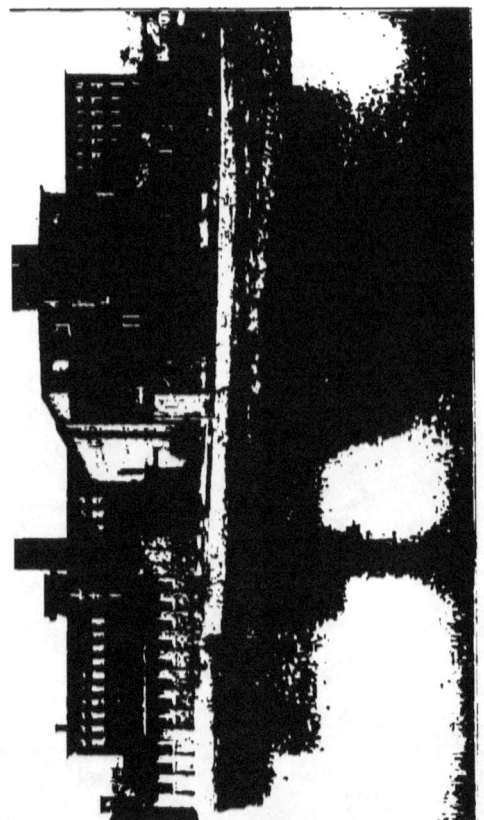

COCHECO MFG. CO.'S MILLS, LOOKING NORTH.

north side of the river, was opened for work in 1881. The old No. 3 was occupied in 1823 and was superseded by the new No. 2 (second section), which began work in 1882. No. 4 was opened in 1825, and No. 5 in its present form, which replaced the old printery in 1850. On March 28, 1877 it was voted to build No. 1 mill and increase the capital stock to $1,500,000. The new No. 1, standing on the south side of Washington street, was finished in 1878.

F. Curtis, who remained until 1834, when Moses Paul became agent. He was succeeded August 1, 1860, by Zimri S. Wallingford, who had been superintendent from 1849, and over the mechanical department for five years previous. Mr. Wallingford was succeeded by John Holland, the present agent, Charles H. Fish, being appointed September 1, 1895.

The first printing of calico in these works was executed under the superintendence of Dr. A. L. Porter, who was suc-

COCHECO MFG. CO., REAR VIEW OF NOS. 2, 3 AND 4 MILLS.

The manufacture of cloth began under the care of John Williams, the first agent. He was the founder of this industry here, and thus of Dover's prosperity. It was his indefatigable activity which turned capital to these falls. Moses Paul was clerk when the works came to the lower falls; John Chase, its first general mechanical superintendent; Andrew Steele, its first master mechanic; Samuel Dunster, the builder of the first practical machinery of the calico printery.

John Williams was succeeded by James

ceeded, before 1830, by John Duxbury, a thoroughly experienced English printer. His successors have been George Mathewson, John Bracewell, Washington Anderton, James Crossley, and the present superintendent, Howard Gray. The original printery was in the present No. 5 mill and other buildings near, but now removed.

It is not possible, in our limited space, to trace in detail the growth of this industry from its small beginning to its present stupendous proportions, nor is that necessary. Men of today are moved most by contact with, and contemplation of, present progressiveness, rather than influenced —save in sentiment—by what has been.

The cotton manufacturing industry of Dover was really a small affair prior to 1827. Up to that time it met with but half-hearted treatment at the hands of men whose foresight did not at once realize the possibilities of the future for this business. The first masterly grasp of the situation which took hold in real earnest to evolve fame for our city and wealth and employment for its citizens was given the

one which in the day of their active privilege labored with that degree of intelligence which lifted not alone themselves, but scores of others to place and fame and comfortable circumstances in life, and provided employment and homes for thousands more.

An idea of the magnitude of this concern can be gleaned from the fact that the plant alone covers an area of over 25 acres, the floor space, devoted exclusively to manufacturing, occupying 30 acres. The company at present operates about

COCHECO MFG. CO. PART OF NO. 2 MILL AND MACHINE SHOP.

cotton industry when the Cocheco Manufacturing Company assumed the control of the mills in 1827. This gave such an impetus to the business that it then became a settled fact that Dover's greatness as a manufacturing centre was assured. From that time dates a progressive march of business prosperity for this company which stands almost, if not entirely, alone in the records of quickly successful response to the intelligently guided methods of manufacturing goods. In years to come the company will be gratefully remembered as

130,000 spindles in 2,800 looms and employs over 2,000 hands constantly. It manufactures in its mills cloths of various kinds, which they print in their extensive print works. The print works contain 16 print machines, with bleachery and finishing mills, with ample accommodation for its product of over 65,000,000 yards of finished cloth per annum. These cloths are all the various printed fabrics now called for by the trade. A large part of the product during the past few seasons has been the finest grades of lawns and

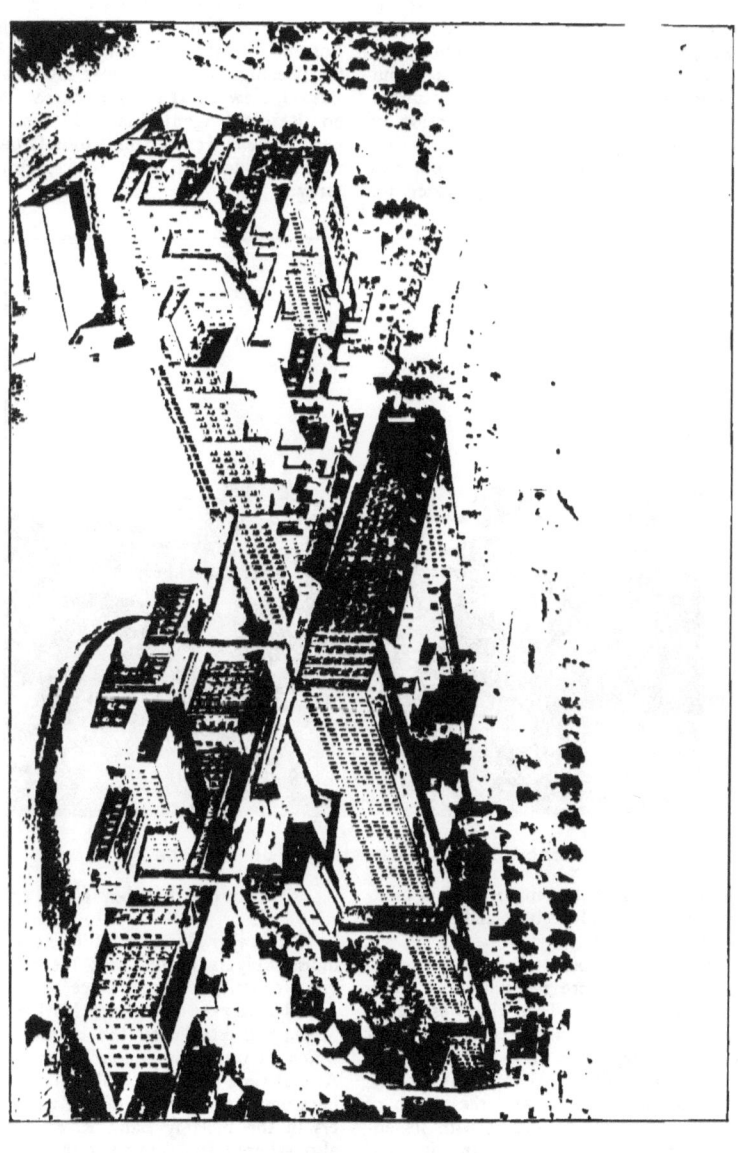

BIRD'S EYE VIEW OF COCHECO MFG. CO.

organdies, which are rapidly taking the place of the fine imported fabrics. The water-power of the Cocheco River furnishes about one-half the power used in the works, the remainder being obtained from steam, in the making of which about 20,000 tons of coal are used yearly under the 45 boilers. In the construction of the mills every care and attention has been given to light and ventilation, and every convenience has been provided for

of prosperity and usefulness even greater than those of its proud record of the past.

The officers of the company are as follows: President, T. Jefferson Coolidge, Boston ; Treasurer, Arthur B. Silsbee, Boston ; Selling agents, Lawrence & Company, Boston, New York, Philadelphia & Chicago ; Resident Agent, Charles H. Fish ; Superintendent of cotton mills, John Drowne ; Superintendent of print works, Howard Gray.

COCHECO MFG. CO. PORTION OF UPPER YARDS.

the well-being of the employees that modern scientific architecture and sanitation has made possible.

The goods manufactured by the company are everywhere recognized as superior in all respects and are widely esteemed by the trade and consumers, the different qualities being standard in all sections of the country. That this important industrial enterprise has reached the zenith of its career no one conversant with its advanced methods will admit, and its constantly increasing reputation for superiority of products gives promise for a future

Sawyer Woolen Mills.

The Sawyer Woolen Mills have been indissolubly associated with the commercial prosperity of Dover since 1824 when Alfred I. Sawyer came from Marlborough, Mass., and established the business from which the present large concern has sprung. At that time the Great Falls Manufacturing Company owned all of the water-powers in the Bellamy Bank River and had also secured land covering the outlet of Chesley's Pond, Barrington, upon which now stands the reservoir dam. In 1845

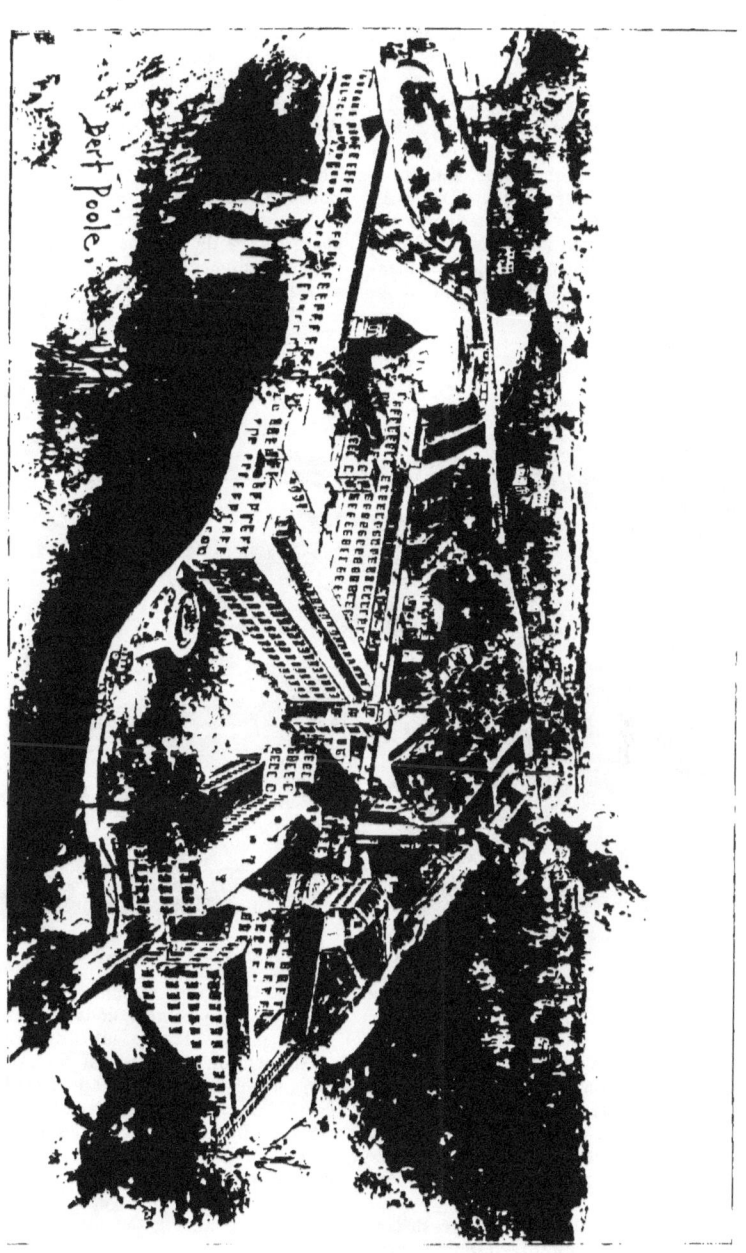

Bert Poole.

BIRD'S EYE VIEW OF SAWYER WOOLEN MILLS.

Mr. Sawyer bought of the Great Falls Manufacturing Company all their rights in the property and continued the business without interruption until his death in 1849. The business then passed to his brother, Zenas Sawyer, 1849-50; Z. and J. Sawyer, 1850-52; F. A. and J. Sawyer (Francis A. Sawyer of Boston, and Jonathan Sawyer of Dover), 1852-1873, when Charles H. Sawyer was admitted, and the concern incorporated as the Sawyer Woolen Mills, with a capital of $600,000. Flannels were exclusively made until 1862,

falls of which is controlled and utilized by the company, as is also the reservoir at Barrington, which was built in 1863-64 and enlarged in 1881, with a capacity of about 450 acres. Tide water reaches to the lower mill and is navigable for coal barges and sloops of moderate capacity. The Portsmouth and Dover branch of the Boston & Maine R. R. has a station at the mills, the freight of which can be discharged directly into the warehouses.

The equipment of the mills is modern and first-class throughout and it is what is

SPINNING ROOM SAWYER WOOLEN MILLS.

when the machinery was gradually changed until 1866, since which attention has been entirely devoted to the manufacture of fine fancy cassimeres, cloths and suitings in the production of which the mills have earned a reputation for quality and durability of goods which is unsurpassed by any similar concern. In 1891 machinery for the manufacture of worsted yarn was added.

The mills are located on the Bellamy River, the water-power of the three lower

called a thirty-nine set mill. These thirty-nine sets of machinery constitute an immense plant. The output of the mills is celebrated for uniformity of texture and elegance of finish, commanding the highest price in the tailoring and clothing trade markets throughout the country. The officers of the company are thoroughly conversant with every detail of the woolen business, and are energetic and wide-awake in advancing the interests of the company.

UPPER MILL AND OFFICES.

PORTION OF THE UPPER MILL.

This enterprise has made of Sawyers—named for the mills—a neat and prosperous village, the prosperity of the company also meaning the prosperity of the community. On an average 600 hands are employed consisting of an unusually high class of operatives.

An average of $20,000 a month is paid out in wages to its employees. This means many comfortable homes and happy families. Adjoining the mills and tastefully laid out on graded streets the company has erected fifty substantially built and comfortable cottages for the families of their employees. These tenements have the best sanitary arrangements and are kept in excellent repair. The company does all in its power to make its employees' lives comfortable and happy and have been

tion of the company and its business added to and conducted by this Company.

The capacity of these two plants proving insufficient for the demands of the increasing business, a third and larger one was erected at Dover, to which place the Somersworth shop was transferred, thereby giving the company two splendidly equipped plants, within a radius of a few miles and simplifying the management of the business to a minimum.

To the Dover plant has been added the extensive business of the John A. White Co. of Concord, manufacturers of all kinds of woodworking machinery, which has attained an enviable reputation in all parts of the world. This company is the most extensive of its kind in the world and through its agencies the machines are

SOMERSWORTH MACHINE COMPANY'S DOVER PLANT.

the prime factor in building up the growing and healthy village which bears its name.

The Somersworth Machine Company.

This Company was incorporated under the laws of New Hampshire in 1848, as the Somersworth Machine Company, and located at Great Falls, now the City of Somersworth.

From a limited business in general jobbing work it soon acquired, under able and progressive management, more than a local reputation and was able to enlarge and broaden all branches of its industry.

The purchase of the Salmon Falls Stove Works was made soon after the founda-

shipped to England, France, Germany, India, Japan, South America, Mexico and Canada. The Japanese Imperial government has purchased several machines and they are also used extensively by the various Japanese railroad companies. The Wm. White Textile Machine Co. of Nashua has also been added. The product of this company is famous all over the country for its excellent wool washing machinery,—dusters, drying machines, steaming and crabbing machines, and other special textile machines. These machines are used in every large and well equipped woolen mill in the country and are also extensively used on the continent of Europe, India and Japan to which places the shipments are increasing. The demand for the machines is phenomenal and keeps the works busy all the time filling the orders.

Besides the manufacture of ranges, heating stoves, furnaces, sinks, hollow ware, etc., at Salmon Falls, and woodworking machinery and textile machinery at Dover, this company are makers of many different kinds of special machinery and pulleys, hangers and shafting, etc.

The main shops of the company are located in Dover and consist of ten buildings, foundry, machine-shops, storehouses, pattern-shops, iron house, coal sheds and stables.

The foundry and workshops are ideal for their separate purposes, being unusually well lighted and ventilated. The buildings are of brick and are very spacious, offering all the advantages to be de-

rooms as well as blacksmith shops, with steam hammers, etc., in connection with them.

The pattern shops, storehouses, coal sheds, iron house and cleaning department are all of sufficient capacity for their respective needs, and the entire plant is lighted by electricity, generated by the company's own dynamos. A spur track runs into the yards from the main tracks of the Western Division of the B. & M. R. R. which pass in the rear of the buildings, thus affording every opportunity for quick and inexpensive freight delivery.

The stove plant wherein are made the world famed Somersworth stoves and ranges is situated at Salmon Falls, three miles from Dover on the Salmon Falls River, about five minutes' walk from the

SOMERSWORTH MACHINE COMPANY'S SALMON FALLS PLANT.

rived from guarantees of safety and convenience for turning out all kinds of first-class work. The equipment throughout is of the highest order, none but the best tools and appurtenances to be found in the market being used.

The foundry is supplied with two large cupolas, one of sixty inches in diameter and another of forty-eight inches, with a melting capacity of 25,000 lbs. per hour, core oven, cranes, and all the paraphernalia to be found in a well equipped establishment. The building proper measures 200 x 60 feet and in connection with it are the core room, foreman's office and supply room, giving the foundry altogether about 20,000 square feet of available floor space. Each of the machine shops contains 15,000 square feet of floor space and have tool and supply

B. & M. station. There are nineteen buildings in all, and the work shops are thoroughly equipped with all the latest improvements for stove manufacture. The quality of the productions in this department being so well known it is useless to elaborate upon them.

Throughout this great industry the plant and appurtenances are of a high order and the machinery comprises all the best and most modern labor saving devices in all departments, by which the expenses of production are reduced to a minimum, thus enabling the company to compete successfully with others as regards quality and also to offer substantial inducements to the trade generally in regard to price, which is always quoted at the lowest possible figure. The products of the company have reached a degree of perfection as regards quality and finish which it is impossible to imagine can be surpassed, and the working of each department is carefully supervised by thoroughly skilled and capable men. With such unsurpassed facilities and advanced methods it is not to be wondered at that the most gratifying success has been achieved, and that the result obtained is of a permanent nature cannot be doubted.

The officers of the company are: President, O. S. Brown; Treasurer, E. H. Gilman; Agent, James C. Sawyer; Directors, O. S. Brown, C. H. Sawyer, E. H. Gil-

Foss and his son, A. Melvin Foss, who came to this city from Strafford where they had been engaged in the grocery and milling business. From its inception the enterprise achieved a notable and well deserved success, securing a firm hold on the favor and patronage of the public which has been greatly strengthened by the lapse of time.

The premises occupied consist of a spacious three story mill 100 x 75 in dimensions fitted up with all the latest improved woodworking tools, machinery and appliances operated by steam power, while

D. FOSS AND SON'S MILL.

man, J. A. White, and J. C. Sawyer. These men are thoroughly experienced business men of undoubted standing, progressive, enterprising and possessing all the attributes so eminently necessary in the upbuilding of this splendid industry. They are men of honor and principle and in financial, commercial and social circles their names are honored and esteemed.

D. Foss and Son.

This business was established in Dover in 1874 by the present partners, Dennis

connected with their mill is an extensive box factory, one of the most complete concerns of the kind in New England. A specialty is made in this department of large packing boxes for the Cocheco Manufacturing Company, the various shoe shops and the trade generally, and a large and constantly increasing business is done. All orders are turned out promptly and in the best possible manner while their estimates in all departments are as low as is consistent with superior materials and workmanship. The firm is a valued feature of the industrial facilities of the city and has a well earned reputation for the ability, energy and honorable character of its management. Mr. Dennis Foss, the senior partner, was born in Strafford seventy-nine years ago and since coming to Dover has made and retained the friendship of our most respected citizens. Mr. A. Melvin Foss, who has the active charge of the business, was born in Strafford in 1847 and received his education at the public and high schools of his native town. He was for two years employed in the grocery store of J. W. Jewell at Strafford which he left to enter his father's store where he remained for seven years, coming to this city with his father to found the present business in 1874. At that time they engaged in the manufacture of boxes and did a general grain business to which was added, ten years ago, the manufacture of doors, sashes and blinds. Mr. Foss served several years as school committee and was elected Mayor of the city in 1893 by a large majority, being re-elected two succeeding years by largely increasing majorities. There is no man in the city more intimately acquainted with its needs and resources, and his experience in public affairs has equipped him with an executive ability sufficient to master every exigency that may arise. He is a director of the Dover Improvement Association and of the Masonic Building Association, Past Master, Strafford Lodge F. and A. M., Past High Priest Belknap Chapter R. A. M., Past Deputy Master of Orphan Council, Eminent Commander St. Paul Commandery, Knights Templar, and Ex-

alted Ruler Dover Lodge of Elks. Mr. Foss is a man of progressive ideas, thoroughly reliable in all his dealings and the success the firm has achieved is of a substantial and lasting character.

United Gas and Electric Company.

In 1887 Mr. H. W. Burgett founded the Dover Electric Company on First Street and in the fall of that year the Fan Cookey Light Company, a small plant in Rochester was also purchased. This was at once changed over and remodeled and the city of Somersworth was poled and wired. In 1888 work was commenced on the New Dam Station on the Salmon Falls river about a mile below Somersworth and the Consolidated Light and Power Company, which superseded the other companies was organized. It was completed in twelve months and at once poled and wired. The same year the Rochester and Somersworth stations were amalgamated with the New Dam Station making one power house for

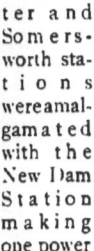
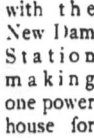
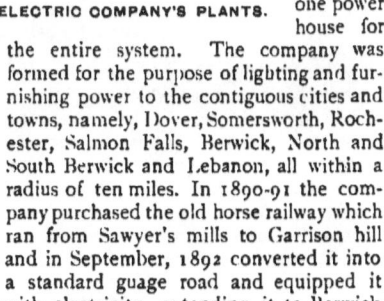

GAS PLANT, DOVER, N.H.

WATER POWER STATION, BERWICK, ME.

UNITED GAS AND ELECTRIC COMPANY'S PLANTS.

the entire system. The company was formed for the purpose of lighting and furnishing power to the contiguous cities and towns, namely, Dover, Somersworth, Rochester, Salmon Falls, Berwick, North and South Berwick and Lebanon, all within a radius of ten miles. In 1890-91 the company purchased the old horse railway which ran from Sawyer's mills to Garrison hill and in September, 1892 converted it into a standard guage road and equipped it with electricity, extending it to Berwick Bridge in Somersworth, a distance of about seven miles. In 1891 the company leased the Dover Gas Light Company for a term of twenty years and furnished electricity and gas light to its patrons. Owing to financial difficulties the company was placed in the hands of a receiver, Jan'y 27, 1894, Wm. F. Brewster being appointed by the court. He was succeeded two months later by H. C. Patterson who acted as receiver for one year. The company was obliged to relinquish the street railway in the spring of 1895 but continued to supply it with power. Hon. H. L. Shepherd of Rockport, Me., was appointed receiver, April 1, 1895 and began the task of straightening out the affairs of the com-

companies in Maine and New Hampshire; John Kivel, Dover, attorney; C. A. Davis, Boston, Mass., Eastern Manager General Electric Co.; Hon. Fred E. Richards, Portland, Me., President Union Mutual Life Ins. Co., President Portland National Bank, President Union Safe Deposit and Trust Co.; Hon. H. L. Shepherd, Rockport, Me., Vice President & General Manager S. E. & H. L. Shepherd Lime Company. Subsequently Hon. Albert Wallace of Rochester was elected president of the company, Hon. H. L. Shepherd, of Rockport, Me., treasurer

THE A. CONVERSE PLACE LUMBER CO.'S BROADWAY MILL.

pany, his first step being to take it out of the hands of a receiver, which was accomplished March 6, 1897. The present incorporated company was then formed under the laws of New Hampshire and Maine and named the United Gas and Electric Company. The following were elected directors: Hon. Albert Wallace, Geo. E. Wallace, Rochester, N. H., firm of E. G. & E. Wallace; Hon. Geo. E. Macomber, Augusta, Me., President of Rockland, Thomaston & Camden Street Railway, and prominently identified with numerous Electric Light and Railway

and general manager and A. D. Richmond, member of the Board of Aldermen of the city of Dover, Gen. Supt. The success of the company under the new management has been most pronounced. Strenuous and well directed efforts have been made to secure new contracts for lighting and the supplying of power with pleasing success. Five hundred arc and 3,000 incandescent lights are now furnished in Dover and surrounding towns and the company's outlook for a future of prosperity is assured. At a meeting of the board of directors held in Dover in May last, it was voted to purchase the extensive water power plant known as the Portsmouth Manufacturing Company of South Berwick, to be utilized in connection with the New Dam Station. This will considerably augment the resources of the company and make the plant one of the best equipped in the state. It will consist of one 2,000 horse-power water, 1,000 horse-power steam, eleven Thompson-Houston fifty arc light dynamos, one 300 K. W. 500 Volt generator and three 350 K. W. three phase 3,120 Volts generators.

the former being equipped with all the latest modern machinery known to the trade. A very heavy stock is at all times carried of Western and Southern pine, oak, ash, mahogany and cherry dressed lumber and a large wholesale demand is supplied, the annual output being between 4,000,000 and 5,000,000 feet, over fifty skilled mechanics and laborers being constantly employed. The company makes a specialty of wood mantels and interior finish and among the contracts they have carried out may be mentioned the interior decoration of Elisha R. Brown's residence, the Wentworth Home, the Chil-

A. CONVERSE PLACE LUMBER CO.'S WHARF AND LUMBER YARDS.

The A. Converse Place Lumber Co.

The A. Converse Place Lumber Company was incorporated in May last, succeeding the firm of Converse & Hammond which was established by Joshua Converse in 1870. The company deals extensively in wholesale and retail lumber and manufactures every description of interior and exterior finish, wood mantels and stair work, their trade extending generally throughout New England and adjoining states. Their offices and yards are situated on Cocheco street and cover an area of six acres with ample wharfage facilities and all requisite conveniences for a successful and systematic conduct of affairs. The mills and branch yard occupy three acres on Broadway,

dren's Home, the Catholic church, Newmarket, the Richardson Dormitory, Hanover, the annex to the Wentworth House, Portsmouth and several others. The officers of the company are: President and General Manager, A. Converse Place; Secretary, Edward M. Horne. Mr. Place was born in Salmon Falls and graduated from the South Berwick Academy in 1886, when he entered the employment of the firm of Converse & Hammond in which he became a partner in 1889. He is thoroughly conversant with every branch of the extensive business he conducts, and under his experienced and conservative management a future of prosperity is assured to the company. He is a Thirty-second Degree Mason, a director of the Co-operative Bank, a member of the

Security Company and represents Ward 3 in the Common Council. In business and social circles he is highly esteemed for his sterling integrity. He is an active member of the Bellamy Club. Mr. Horne is a native of Somersworth and a graduate of the High School of that city. He was bookkeeper for the Dover Clothing Company until 1894, in which year he accepted a similar position with

Dover Furniture Co.

One of the best and most prominent furniture establishments in this part of the state, carrying the largest and most complete stock, is that of the Dover Furniture Company. The premises occupied for the business embrace a substantial four-story and basement building at the corner of Third and Chestnut streets, opposite

DOVER FURNITURE COMPANY'S WAREHOUSE.

Converse & Hammond. In addition to his secretarial duties Mr. Horne represents the company on the road and has established an enviable reputation for his honorable dealings and business-like methods. He is most popular among a large circle of friends who esteem him for his many excellent qualities. Mr. Horne is Master Mason of Moses Paul Lodge and a member of the Bellamy Club.

the Boston & Maine depot, each floor measuring 40x100 feet and of easy access by means of the elevator. The stock shown is as complete as modern methods demand. It comprises all the latest novelties and prevailing styles in artistic home furnishings, parlor, library, dining-room and chamber furniture; carpets, rugs, floor cloths, portieres, draperies, pictures and everything, in fact, in high grade and medium house furnishings for the mansion or cottage. The success of the house from its inception in 1892 has been most pronounced and their trade is very large, people coming from the adjoining towns, within a radius of thirty miles to purchase their house furnishing goods from this well known house. From ten to twelve courteous assistants are constantly employed and three teams are kept busy delivering orders.

The business was founded, in 1892, by the present partners, J. Everett Ewer, and J. Eugene Mooney, both of whom are

Mr. Ewer was born at Week's Mills, Me., and took a collegiate course at the Gardner High School. During his school days, and for a couple of years afterwards, he engaged in journalism and then spent ten years in the saddlery hardware furnishing business in Providence, R. I., which he left to form the present partnership. He is a Thirty-Second degree Mason, Moses Paul Lodge, A. F. and A. M., a member of Providence Chapter, Orphan Council, Dover, St. John's Commandery, Providence, and Rhode Island Consistory, S. P. R. S.

AN INTERIOR VIEW DOVER FURNITURE COMPANY.

thoroughly conversant with its every detail and are capable and progressive business men who have made a close study of successfully catering to the public requirements. In this lies the success they have achieved.

Among the recent furnishing contracts carried out by this firm may be mentioned the complete furnishing of the Wentworth Home for the aged, several cottages and hotels at York Beach, Wells Beach and other seashore resorts, the hotels at Milton Three Ponds, Gonic, Epping and the Granite State Park Hotel.

Mr. Mooney is a native of Whitefield, Me., where he was born in 1870. He was educated in the public school of his native town, afterwards taking courses at the Pittston Academy and Augusta Business College. Upon completing his education he engaged in the furniture business with Messrs. Preble and Keene, Gardner, Me., where he remained three years, afterwards accepting the position of manager for the Portsmouth Furniture Company which he left to engage in his present enterprise. He is a member of the Bellamy Club, a member of Moses Paul Lodge,

A. F. and A. M. and the Dover Lodge of Elks.

Both partners are highly esteemed in business and social circles, are young, ambitious but conservative in their methods, and to this and their intimate acquaintance with business methods may be ascribed the success they have achieved.

Thomas H. Dearborn & Co.

A history of the business interests of Dover would not be complete without nearly every business man in the city who prognosticated that such an extensive establishment could not be made a success in Dover but nothing daunted they took the step. Five years later they added nearly as much more room, and a well equipped cloak room was opened. Two years ago they took the basement in which they opened a kitchen furnishing department. The rapid growth of this house can be attributed to the same cause which has made the success of all large concerns, perseverance, energy and honest dealings combined with hard work,

RESIDENCE OF THOMAS H. DEARBORN, SILVER STREET.

reference to the dry goods and department store of Thomas H. Dearborn & Co. which was established by the present partners Thomas H. Dearborn and Frank N. French in 1884. From a small beginning this establishment has grown to be second to none of its kind in this section. Upon first coming to Dover they purchased the dry goods business located in the store 470 Central Avenue. Two years later an opportunity presented itself to secure what is now a part of the present large concern. This step was taken against the judgment and advice of a liberal use of printer's ink and keeping faith with the public.

Thos. H. Dearborn was born in Northfield, N. H., in 1860. He received his education at Exeter and New Hampton and upon leaving school engaged in the dry goods business in Exeter. Subsequently he went to Texas and was engaged in raising sheep and horses, finally coming to Dover to engage in his present business. He is a conservative but enterprising business man who has attained his present position by merit alone. Mr. Dearborn is a member of Moses Paul

THOMAS H. DEARBORN.

FRANK N. FRENCH.

THOMAS H. DEARBORN & CO.'S STORE.

Lodge F. & A. M., the Royal Arcanum, an Elk, and Redman, and is a deservedly popular citizen of wide acquaintance and great influence in the business life of the city, being president of the Dover Commercial Club. Frank N. French was born in Exeter, in 1860 and graduated from Exeter Academy, subsequently taking a business course at the New Hampton Commercial College. He was engaged in the dry goods business in his native city until he came to Dover and formed the present partnership. Mr. French is a Mason, a member of the Bellamy Club and is most highly thought of by the community at large.

Dover Business College.

With the young man of ambition the question above all others is how to get a start. In order to secure a foothold somewhere he must be able to do some-

THOMAS M. HENDERSON,
Principal Dover Business College.

thing useful. The Dover Business College course of study is designed to qualify the prospective business man to cope with the difficulties he is sure to meet. It gives thorough and scientific training in those things that the business proprietor and manager should be thoroughly familiar with, and without which he will be constantly handicapped in his business career. The College was founded on the principle that permanent success in business, as elsewhere, must be based upon adequate preparation. The Dover Business College furnishes the training and preparation that fit young men and women to achieve success which would otherwise be long deferred if not actually unattainable. The College has earned a reputation for efficiency in helping young people on the road to success. It puts them in possession of a practical business education; it assists its graduates to responsible and lucrative positions; its course of study and training and the association with its capable teachers and energetic business students give an incentive to effort and an impulse to ambition. The College was founded in October, 1896, by Bliss Brothers of Conneaut, O., Mr. T. M. Henderson being appointed principal. In July, 1897, Mr. Henderson acquired the business which he conducted under the original name until last January when the title became as at present. The class-rooms are located in the Odd Fellows block and consist of five spacious rooms excellently equipped for business purposes, the main class-room measuring 40x60 feet. The students have the advantage of working in a well appointed business office which also contains a First and Second National Bank thus making them thoroughly conversant with every detail of business life. The prescribed courses of study are classed as Commercial, Shorthand and Practical English. The Commercial Course is designed to furnish a thorough preparation for a successful business career. It gives a complete course in the science and mechanical work of bookkeeping and all its collateral branches, the Williams and Rogers System being adopted. In the Shorthand classes the Dement-Pitman System is used, being the very latest development of the world-famed Pitman method. This is a very strong feature of the College as shown by the responsible positions now being held by some of the graduates in the Shorthand department.

MAIN CLASS ROOM, DOVER BUSINESS COLLEGE.

The department of business practice and the Counting-room department are the crowning features of the College—those which have contributed to its reputation for thoroughness and efficiency. The pupil here becomes in all essentials a practical business man. Night sessions are held on Mondays, Wednesdays and Fridays at which the same course is taken as in the day classes and students are graduated on completing their course.

Mr. Henderson was born in Pickering, Ont., Canada, in 1861, receiving his early education at the Whitly High School. He subsequently took a course at Pickering College and obtained a professional teacher's certificate from the Toronto Normal School. He afterwards graduated from the Central Business College, Toronto. His teaching experience extends over a period of twelve years, in both Public Schools and Business College work. When Bliss Brothers founded their School in this city he was chosen principal and is today sole proprietor of the Dover Business College. Mr. Henderson is well-grounded in and thoroughly familiar with every particular of business as practiced in the best Commercial offices, and the success the College has attained under his skilful and capable management is as pleasing as it is pronounced.

— •

Hon. John Tapley Welch.

Hon. John Tapley Welch, who assumed charge of the Post Office May 24, 1898, is widely known in this section, has held many positions of trust and is recognized as a man of abundant executive ability. The appointment of Postmaster was secured by Mr. Welch after a long and exciting contest.

Mr. Welch was born in Dover, December 15, 1856, and was educated in the public schools of Dover and at Dartmouth College. After completing his education he devoted many years to newspaper work. He served as city editor of the Whiteside Sentinel of Morrison, Ill., the Dover Daily Republican and Dover Daily Times, and was for several years the Dover correspondent of the Boston Globe.

He has had much experience in a clerical capacity, having been clerk of the Dover police court in 1881-1882, register of probate for Strafford county from 1882 to 1887, five years a member and first secretary of the board of trustees of the Dover Public Library, and from February 1890, to July 1894, was chief time clerk of the government printing office at Washington. Mr. Welch represented Ward 3 in the legislature of 1889, and served as clerk of the committee on railroads.

He has always been an ardent Republican and an active supporter of his party.

HON. JOHN T. WELCH,
Postmaster of Dover.

He has been a delegate to every Republican state and district convention since 1882, is at present a member of the republican state committee and has been a member of the Dover Ward 3 committee for several years. He also served as supervisor of elections during the presidental election of 1884.

In 1896 he was unanimously nominated for Senator in the 22nd Senatorial district and was elected by the largest majority ever given in the district. In the Senate he was chairman of the committee on revision of laws and also served on the committees on education, roads, bridges, canals, and manufactures.

Mr. Welch is a member of the New Hampshire Historical Society, the Dover Historical Society, the Sons of the American Revolution and the following secret societies in Dover: Mt. Pleasant lodge and Prescott Encampment, I. O. O. F.; Olive Branch Lodge, K. of P.; Wanalanset Tribe of Red Men; Coeur de Lion Castle. K. G. E., and Dover Lodge 184, B. P. O. E.

The Late Levi Gerrish Hill, M. D.

For half a century Dr. Hill was identified with Dover; his interest and activity never flagging from the time of his coming in 1848, to his death in 1898.

To the most remarkable degree he escaped the infirmities of age, continuing his

THE LATE DR. LEVI GERRISH HILL.

professional duties to within one month of his decease. His tall figure and stately courtesy seemed a part of Dover.

Dr. Hill was a thorough New Englander, whose ancestors were conspicuous in the early history of the colony: Elder Hatevil Nutter, Thomas Leighton, John Hill of New Hampshire, Henry Sewall, Stephen Dummer and Captain William Gerrish of Massachusetts were his grandfathers in the 17th century. Chief Justice Samuel Sewall was his kinsman, and also Lt. Gov. William Dummer. He was the son of Andrew Neal and Sally (Leighton) Hill and was born in Strafford, N. H., July 7th, 1812.

His boyhood was spent on his father's farm—attending the district school till the age of fifteen, after which he attended Newmarket and Gilmanton Academies.

Deciding upon the medical profession he attended three full courses of lectures at Dartmouth Medical College and was graduated therefrom in 1838.

The degree of A. M. was conferred upon him by Dartmouth College in 1883.

Immediately after graduation Dr. Hill began practice at Salisbury, N. H. Two years later he established himself in Norfolk, Va., where resided his only brother, Capt. Andrew Leighton Hill. In Norfolk he acquired a good practice but his fondness for New England impelled him to return to New Hampshire.

The Medical Societies of the City, County and State, had in Dr. Hill an active and progressive member. He was president of the New Hampshire Medical Society in 1869, and president of its board of trustees from the establishment of that Board. He was president of the Dover Medical Society in 1854; president of the Strafford District Medical Society in 1862; permanent member of the American Medical Association; vice president in 1881; president of the Examining Board under the registration law of New Hampshire during the first ten years of its existence, 1878 to 1888; honorary member of the Portsmouth Medical Society, and of the Maine Medical Association.

On November 13th, 1893, he was elected president of the Dartmouth Alumni Association of S. E. New Hampshire.

Dr. Hill was a Mason—member of Strafford Lodge since June, 1856. In November, 1849, he joined the Wecohamet Lodge of Odd Fellows. He joined

served on the field as captain of the Thirty-fifth Massachusetts infantry; Adelaide Shackford, wife of Rev. James M. Buckley, LL.D., of Morristown, N. J.; and Margaret Leighton, deceased, wife of Seth M. Milliken of New York city.

Late Joseph Dame Guppey.

Capt. James Guppey was born in Beverly, Mass., in 1732, and came to Dover while young to be educated for a nautical career, and at the age of twenty-one commanded a ship. He sailed from Portsmouth, N. H., and Salem, Mass., his family residing in Portsmouth. In 1767 he

RESIDENCE OF THE LATE DR. HILL, WASHINGTON STREET.

the First Parish church of Dover, May 6, 1877.

Dr. Hill was married July 30, 1838, to Abigail Burnham, daughter of the late Samuel Shackford, Esq., a woman of remarkable beauty and strength of character, whose death on October 25th, 1895, was deeply mourned by a wide circle.

Their children are: Clara A., wife of the late George F. French, A.M., M.D., of Minneapolis, Minn., surgeon United State volunteers and personal staff surgeon of Gen. U. S. Grant; Abby A., wife of Maj. William N. Meserve, then in command of Forts Barnard and Albany, near Washington, D. C., having previously

purchased the Capt. Heard farm in Dover, and after repairing the house, which was built in 1690, removed his family there. When our independence was established he relinquished a sea-faring life and retired to his farm. In August 1782, the government sent him to the friendly French fleet on our coast as a competent and trustworthy pilot. He piloted five of the fleet to Portsmouth harbor and remained with them three months as the confidential business advisor of Marquis de Vandreuil. He died in 1826, aged ninety-three years, leaving his farm to his son John, who was born in 1768 and died in 1855, aged eighty-seven years. John had five sons; two died in early manhood, of the other three Gen. J. J. Guppey of

February 11, 1823. He received a good common school education supplemented

THE OLD GUPPEY HOUSE (BUILT 1690), PORTLAND STREET.

Wisconsin, a graduate of Dartmouth, died in 1893, aged seventy-three years. The next one, Joseph D., died in Dover in 1890. The youngest, Jeremy B., owns the homestead farm, and with his two sisters, Mrs. Abby G. Trafton and Miss Hannah G. Guppey, occupies the same house built in 1690 that his grandfather and father occupied so many years.

Joseph Dame Guppey was born in Dover,

by a special academic course in mathematics. He inherited the family physique, and was a sound, practical man, always ready to give a strong, common-sense opinion upon any subject to which his attention had been called. In early life he succeeded as a school teacher, and his fellow-citizens repeatedly showed their confidence in his integrity and ability by placing him in positions of public trust

THE LATE EX-MAYOR JOSEPH D. GUPPEY.

and responsibility, auditor, moderator, school committeeman, county commissioner, member of the Constitutional convention and mayor in 1879-1880. He retired from each office with honor and credit. It may be briefly added that ex-Mayor Guppey was a good type of that useful class of citizens who are always safe advisors in critical times or in an emergency of any kind.

Hon. Hosea Ballou Perkins.

Hon. Hosea Ballou Perkins was born in Dover August 4, 1819, and is the son of Robert Perkins and Relief Earle. He has the distinction of belonging to one of the oldest and most honored families of New Hampshire. His ancestors were men who made history and there are in Dover today the old mansions built by these men, which are now some of our time-honored reminders of days and people that have passed from all but memory.

Mr. Perkins received his education in the public schools of New Hampshire and throughout his school days showed the greatest aptitude for acquiring knowledge and improving his opportunities.

Leaving school at the early age of fourteen, he divided the remaining years of his boyhood between farm and clerk

HON. HOSEA BALLOU PERKINS.

life, going to New York City when seventeen years old with no capital save his native energy and tact, and without an acquaintance in the metropolis except a poor colored man.

He began his business life in New York as a clerk in the well-known carpet establishment of Shaw & Carter. At the end of his second year he refused a liberal salary from this company and embarked in business for himself, taking for a partner his younger brother, James P. Perkins. For twenty-five years the career of this firm of carpet merchants was one continued success in spite of the financial crisis through which our country passed during that time.

During the last year of Fernando Wood's mayoralty of New York the nomination for the assembly in the Twelfth Ward was tendered Mr. Perkins and declined. Later, under the leadership of John Kelly, he was nominated for State Senator, but refused the nomination, much to the regret of his party.

Mr. Perkins has been a life long Democrat, efficient and active on the stump, during many campaigns. He never sought any political office, but was content to serve the educational interests of the city for more than thirty years as Commissioner and Inspector of Public Schools.

In 1871 Mr. Perkins received the honorary degree of Master of Arts from Bowdoin and in 1875 from Dartmouth College. It was in the fall of '75 that he delivered to the Dartmouth students his popular lecture on Robert Burns, the Scottish poet, which was repeated two years later at the request of the faculty. Mr. Perkins has delivered many addresses before agricultural societies, colleges, political and other gatherings, also before lyceums in different parts of the country. As an after-dinner speaker he has always been in great demand. During the Civil War he represented his native state in the New England Relief Association, pleading eloquently the cause of the Union.

When the Second New Hampshire regiment arrived in New York under the command of Colonel Marston, Mr. Perkins was selected by the sons of New Hampshire, resident in this city, to make the address of welcome, which he did on the Battery in the presence of ten thousand people, and the address was published in several of the New England papers.

The following is an extract from one of Mr. Perkins' addresses before the Board of Education of New York City : " I had hardly been in this Board one month when a gentleman well known in this community, holding a high social position, but not especially noted for his liberality, said to me : ' Commissioner, I think public education is a failure.' I answered him that if he entertained such an idea it was a delusive dream that enwrapped his senses, an idle fancy sporting with his fears. And let me say here, to-night, in the presence of this Board and of the intelligent members of the press and of all, that the common school here in this great city, amid the bleak hills of New England, or on the broad prairies of the far distant west, is no more a failure than ' popular liberty, constitutional law, or the Christian religion.' The past is full of its great achievements, the future will acknowledge its sovereign power.

The common school a failure ! Why, sir, you might as well attempt to dam up the waters of Niagara with cobwebs as to try to fetter the feet of the noble men and women who are engaged in the grand work of popular instruction in this great, free and prosperous republic, whose very foundations rest upon the intelligence and virtue of the people.

From our public schools and our colleges are to go out into the world the men and the women who are to make states and form our national strength, who are to still further illustrate the grand idea that man is capable of self-government, endowed by his Maker with natural rights older than the sceptre of the king, and that can be taken from him only by that Omnipotent Power ' to whom a thousand years are but as yesterday when it is past,' and who controls the destinies of men and nations.

Look back, oh illiberal and misguided opponent of public education, through the mist and haze of the past, and tell me if you can what paintings of Apollos, what statutes of Phidias, what poems of Homer or Virgil are half as noble, or have contributed half as much to the general welfare and prosperity of mankind as the humble little temple of learning embosomed amid the pine forests of Maine, or standing upon the bleak shores of Erie or Ontario.

Lord Bacon suggested to the people of Great Britain a system of public education, but the titled, tinselled and courtly throng of that period did not think it safe, under their form of government, to educate the masses, and they rejected Bacon's plan, and ' like the base Judean, they threw a rich pearl away.' But to-day has changed the picture !—the people of Great Britain are proud of their public schools, and public education engrosses the attention of her best and brightest intellects. If people living under a monarchical government are taking so much interest in the education of the masses, why talk of public education being a failure in this glorious land of ours, where every man can rise in the majesty of his own intellect and where the avenues to knowledge, distinction and power are clear and broad for all.

But, Mr. President, if our great system of education be ever destroyed by antagonists of whatever name (I allude to no particular sect or faction), I, for one, can-

not but think its light will linger even
when its sun is set, gilding the loftiest
spires of our land with the departing glo-
ries of a system that now commands the
admiration of the young, the generous and
the good.

Our public schools, to-day, are better
organized and equipped and are doing
better work than at any previous period
in their history. Let us then, whether in
this Board or out of it, give to them our
counsel, our means and our best efforts.
Let us plead for education in all lands
and among all people, and when education shall have become
universal, may we not
hope for that happy
epoch for which the
good have so long
prayed, and the war-
rior's battered panoply
shall be laid aside.
Then will peace, the
blessed angel of peace,
be crowned with tri-
umphant garl a n d s ;
then, in the eloquent
language of another
' will dim Meroe shout
freedom from beyond
the fountains of the
Nile, and lips as stony
as the sphinx will
preach the Gospel ' of
the better day."

Mr. Perkins is a
member of the Tam-
many society, Demo-
cratic club, Fordham
club, and has been
president of the Wash-
ington Heights Century club for the past
ten years.

On November 9, 1843, Mr. Perkins
was united in marriage to Harriet Louise
Hanmer and their children were Edwin
Earle, who died in 1893, Harriet Ida,
Helen Hanmer, James P., Jr., who died
in 1851, Lucy Charlotte, died in 1853,
Mary Grace and Robert Randolph.

Probably no man in New York is better known in society or among the habitues
of the rides and drives than is Mr. Perkins.
Although he has attained more than the

usual number of years allowed to the average man, of even the most robust health,
Mr. Perkins is active, energetic and
sparkling with the spirit of vigorous manhood. No social gathering is quite complete without his presence. He has enjoyed the friendship of some of the greatest men of the metropolis, past and present, and his beautiful residence amid the
trees of Washington Heights is fragrant
with memories of these men who have
from time to time enjoyed the stately but
cordial hospitality which is a pleasing feature of his home life.

James E. Hayes.

JAMES E. HAYES,
Sheriff, Strafford County.

James E. Hayes
was born April 13,
1840, on the old
homestead at Farming-
ton, which his great-
grandfather, D a n i e l
Hayes, cleared from
the wilderness. The
homestead was also the
birthplace of Daniel
Hayes, Jr., the grand-
father, and of his son,
Richard Hayes, the
father of the subject of
this sketch. Richard
Hayes married Martha
A. Edgerly of Far-
mington, who bore him
two children, Annie
M. Hayes, who mar-
ried Alvah M. Kimball,
and James E. Hayes.
In 1882 Mr. Hayes
erected, in his native
town, a factory for the
manufacture of heels for boots and shoes,
which is now in charge of his son, Eugene
B. Hayes. The marked popularity of Mr.
Hayes was attested in the flattering vote
by which he was chosen to his present responsible position in 1895. For many
years he had served as a Deputy Sheriff
and his appointment to the position of
Sheriff of Strafford County was but
a just tribute to his merit. Although practically a stranger to public functions, Mr.
Hayes' incumbency of the sheriff's office
has been an eminently able one, the many

problems constantly arising in connection with his multifarious duties being handled with care and discretion. Mr. Hayes also acts as Keeper of the Jail. In politics he is a firm supporter of Republican principles, having cast his first vote for Abraham Lincoln. · He represented the town of Farmington in the state legislature in 1872 and in 1887 was elected selectman of the town. He was married Nov. 24, 1870, to Miss Mary E. Peavey of Farmington, a daughter of John L. and Emily Furber Peavey, and has two sons, Eugene B. Hayes, deputy sheriff, and manager of his heel factory at Farmington, and John R. Hayes, a student.

Union Electric Railway.

This company which now controls the street transportation of passengers in Dover and vicinity is well worthy of extended notice in this work. Its growth has been marvellous and in complete harmony with the progress of the age, providing unrivalled facilities for public pleasure and convenience.

When in the early part of 1882 the idea of a street railway was first conceived by Mr. Harrison Haley it was looked upon as a wild scheme, too much for the little city of Dover, but, notwithstanding the opposition and ridicule of the enterprise, by the perseverance of Mr. Haley the necessary capital, $20,000, was subscribed by liberal and public-spirited citizens who at that time had no assurance of ever receiving any return for the money subscribed, but were confident it would be a great public good. It did, however, pay dividends.

The building of the road between Sawyer's and Garrison Hill was commenced in the spring of 1882 the work being pushed on so rapidly that by the following July the first cars were run over the new road, a distance of two and one-half miles.

The old road succeeded for some years and was greatly appreciated, but the great development of electricity showed the futility of attempting to run cars on antiquated principles while the new power of electricity could be procured upon favorable terms. The consequence has

been that the horse-cars have given place entirely to the modern and expensively fitted trolley-cars; and the application of electricity as a motive power has contributed much to the convenience of the traveling public.

Since the formation of the present company the management has been constantly making improvements and the change has been decidedly beneficial to Dover. The entire roadbed between Sawyer's Mills and the city of Somersworth, the terminals of the line, has been rebuilt and new sixty-foot sixty-pound steel rails laid. In the city limits a steel girder rail has been employed which can be paved with granite blocks between the tracks. The cost of this improvement, including labor and auxiliary expenses, has been very great. But the inestimable benefits derived from a well-equipped railway like ours are practical as well as sentimental. Suburbs are opened up and made more accessible from the city, thereby diffusing the population, improving the health of the people and largely increasing the number of house owners.

One of the greatest attractions of the road is Central Park, which is situated on the line of the Union Electric Railway, midway between the cities of Dover and Somersworth, and contains twenty acres of hill and dale, woodland and plain. Bounded on the west by Lake Willand, a body of water called in the land grants "The Great Pond," and as early as 1674 named "Cochecho Pond," or "the pond of the Cochecho." The Indian tribe who massacred Maj. Waldron and burned the garrison over his body at Dover, June 27, 1689, often tented around this sheet of water as a fishing ground.

The air at the Park is of the purest and best. A good, cool breeze can be enjoyed there in the hottest of weather. The scenery around the lake is beautiful. A fleet of boats is there, and a party can spend an hour in pleasure rowing and sailing about the lake, or, if they do not care to row or sail, they can charter a steam launch at a very small expense, and the trip around the lake is a most delightful one.

This Park has all of the accompaniments required for first-class grounds for picnic or excursion parties. There is a large Casino building, 50 x 150 feet, two stories, containing a large banquet hall and kitchen on the lower floor, and a fine exhibition hall above. Also a Pavilion, 50 x 150 feet, which can be used for meetings, entertainments, dances, etc. A lawn tennis ground, suitably enclosed, and a base ball and foot ball ground, with an amphitheatre of 1500 seats, gives a splendid opportunity for either of these popular games. There is also a fine track for bicycle races. The grounds are

than this delightful resort. It is of easy access, and excursion parties over the Boston & Maine R. R., Portsmouth and Dover, and Northern divisions of the Boston & Maine can be furnished with electric cars from Dover and Somersworth to the Park. The proprietors of the Park have expended large sums to make it the most attractive possible. Arrangements can be made for reduced transportation over all the divisions of Boston & Maine road for picnics and excursions. The use of the Park is free to all picnic and excursion parties. Information relative to

INTERIOR FURBER AND WIGGIN'S STORE.

lighted by electricity, are furnished with seats, swings, picnic tables, etc. Ice water tanks are well distributed over the grounds throughout the summer season. The walks and grounds are in fine condition. No liquors are sold in or around the Park. An efficient police will also see to it that no disorder is permitted. Churches and societies in the surrounding towns which are to hold picnics the coming season should not forget that Central Park is one of the most delightful spots to be found in New England. Here every convenience is supplied, and there is no place better adapted for pleasure parties

the Park and Electric Railway can be obtained of H. C. Weston, Superintendent.

The following are the directors of the company :—Sumner Wallace, Albert Wallace, Geo. S. Wallace, James E. Lothrop, Harrison Haley. President, Sumner Wallace ; Vice President, Geo. E. Wallace ; Treasurer, Harry Hough ; Superintendent, H. C. Weston.

D. L. Furber and Wiggin.

The manufacture of ladies' and gents' fine hand-sewed boots and shoes in Dover was begun by Mr. D. L. Furber in 1884 in his present factory, rear of 101 Washington Street, and under his intelligent direction the enterprise has been guided on to a highly successful and prosperous career, the output increasing annually and keeping fifteen hands constantly employed. Mr. Furber is the inventor of Furber's Patent Elastic Band Bicycle shoes which have become so popular with wheelmen and also manufactures golf, football and sporting footwear for the trade. He personally supervises all the processes of construction and his practical experience in the business enables him to secure perfect production. The best materials, leather, findings, etc. are utilized and the entire output of the factory is custom work and unexcelled for genuine merit, being unsurpassed for finish, style and lasting qualities. The factory measures 60 x 20 feet and is well equipped with heel-finishing and other special machinery for the proper carrying on of the business, and is lighted by electricity. In March last Mr. Furber admitted Mr. C. F. Wiggin to partnership when the style of the firm became as at present. In the retail store located at the same address and facing on Washington Street, the products of the factory are retailed and an excellent and ever growing demand has been created for these goods. The partners are men of large business capacity and practical experience who have made the shoe industry a life study. They are highly esteemed in trade circles for their skill and just methods and have built up a business alike creditable to their industry and enterprise.

The E. Morrill Furniture Co.

For over half a century the name of Morrill has been associated with the furniture trade in Dover, the original business having been founded by E. Morrill in the same building where the present concern is located.

In 1886 Henry J. Grimes and Charles E. Cate acquired the business which is centrally located in the five story building 93 Washington street, four buildings in all being utilized with a total floor space of 29,-900 square feet. The house bears an excellent reputation for the superiority of its goods and the honorable character of its management. Through the energy and application of the partners in catering to the requirements of their patrons they have developed and retained a patronage of the most desirable nature, extending throughout this and the surrounding counties and each year sees their popularity

THE E. MORRILL FURNITURE CO.'S STORE.

and entire trade increase. The establish·ment is fitted up in the most approved style, with every convenience for the accommodation and display of goods and the reception of customers. The immense stock carried is well worthy of examination, representing as it does the products of the leading manufacturers of the kind in the country. The assortment embraces elegant parlor suits, chairs and lounges, chamber suits in profuse variety, hall, library, office and kitchen furniture, draperies, carpets, mattings, rugs, and upholstery goods. The firm make a specialty of the manufacturing and upholstering of fine parlor furniture, ten skilled men being constantly employed. Both a jobbing and retail trade is carried on and customers can at all times depend upon receiving the best goods at the lowest price the market affords.

The partners are both natives of this city where they also received their education, Mr. Cate subsequently taking a course at the New Hampton Business College. They have both received a thorough and practical business experience which they apply intelligently in the furthering of their patrons' interests. Mr. Grimes is a member of the Dover Lodge of Elks and Mr. Cate belongs to the I. O. O. F.

The Shoe Industry.

The making of shoes for the Southern and Western markets has come to be recognized as a leading and fast growing industry in the city. Employment is afforded to several hundred of our citizens in the different shoe shops and their location in our city has added to its prestige as a great manufacturing centre.

Almost every variety of footwear is manufactured here, and every device that would add beauty to appearance or comfort in the wearing has been studied out and adopted by the local manufacturers.

The concentration of skilled labor at certain points, in obedience to forces that cannot always be defined, but which can never be successfully opposed, has made possible the origin and growth of the industrial centres of New England. The business of shoemaking once well estab-lished here, the dictates of convenience, economy and good business management alike suggest to the manufacturer the advantage of pursuing it in Dover.

J. H. IRELAND & CO.

The business of this representative concern was founded in 1894 by J. H. Ireland, E. P. Dodge and H. B. Little and under their intelligent direction the enterprise has been guided to a successful and highly prosperous career. The fine building occupied for the business was erected by the Dover Improvement Association. It is a five story brick building measuring 250 x 50 feet and is equipped in admirable style with modern improved machinery, operated by steam power, and in the various departments of work employment is given to 400 skilled hands. The company manufactures women's and misses' shoes of medium grade, the capacity of the factory being seventy-five sixty-pair cases a day. Mr. Wm. H. Mathews is superintendent of the factory and his practical experience as a shoemaker enables him to secure perfect production in all departments. The trade of the concern extends generally throughout the United States and the annual volume of transactions shows a steady increase each succeeding year.

CHARLES H. MOULTON & CO.

Thirteen years ago this business was inaugurated in Dover by L. W. Nute & Co., but upon the death of Mr. Nute in 1888 Mr. Charles H. Moulton became proprietor and about one year ago admitted Mr. W. H. Moody into partnership. The premises occupied were built by the Dover Improvement Association. They are spacious in size, the factory being a four story wooden structure measuring 150 x 50 feet, with a storehouse 100 x 50 feet in dimensions. The various departments are equipped with the latest improved tools, machinery and appliances known to the trade. Two hundred hands are employed in turning out men's heavy pegged and nailed shoes, creedmoors and ties which find a ready market in the south and west. The products of the shop are all of the best quality and workmanship and none but first class hands are employed in their manufacture. Mr. F. J. Boyden is superintendent of the factory and is a thoroughly practical man who is acquainted with every detail of the business. He has resided in Dover for the past thirty-three years and is deservedly popular.

THE BRADLEY-SAYWARD SHOE CO.

This company are manufacturers of men's, youths' and boys' shoes, and can justly lay claim to the careful attention of the trade throughout the country. The company was incorporated in November, 1897, under the above title, the previous firm name, since its inception twenty years ago, having been Bradley & Sayward. The present officers are J. Bradley, Hudson, Mass., president, and H. S. Sayward, Cambridge, Mass., secretary and treasurer. The company has met with pleasing success, owing largely to the fact of their producing all the latest and most approved styles in boots and shoes including men's heavy work, bals, creedmoors and ties, and the introduction of better methods in their manufacture. The factory consists of a four story building measuring 40 x 60 feet, thoroughly equipped with the latest machinery and appliances, and having a productive capacity of 600 pairs of shoes a day. Constant employment is given to a force of between fifty and sixty skilled operatives. The product of the factory finds a ready market, being noted for superior workmanship and finish, having all the elements of durability with the added advantage of easy fit and attractive appearance. Mr. E. I. Bennett is superintendent and is a thoroughly practical shoemaker, conversant with all the details of the business.

J. H. HURD & SON.

This business was originally established at Farmington in 1850 by John H. Hurd, who subsequently removed it to Dover over a quarter of a century ago. The partners are John H. Hurd and Clarence I. Hurd, who personally superintend the details of the business. The firm manufacture split and grain brogans, plow shoes, creedmoors and Dom Pedros, all their work being standard screw and pegged, for which they possess every facility in the way of special machinery and equipment. The plant comprises a three story building 100 x 50 feet in dimensions and the output is 500 pairs a day, fifty hands being employed. Mr. J. H. Hurd is much esteemed in business circles and is a trustee of the Strafford Savings Bank. The house ships its goods to the southern and western markets and also exports to South Africa.

DOVER HEEL COMPANY.

This concern does a large business in the manufacture of heels for men's boots and shoes. The premises are ample for the requirements of the business and are equipped with all the latest and most approved machinery known to the trade. About twenty hands are constantly employed and the output of the shop increases yearly.

The Boston & Maine Railroad.

The importance of railroads cannot be ignored in this era of progressiveness, nor can they be relegated to a minor position by any community aspiring to modern methods. In its intermediate relations with the Union at large, a city must grant railway communication equal consideration with all other systems of transportation, for to this medium more than all others yet devised by man's ingenuity is due the present advanced state of civilization throughout the world.

The Boston & Maine Railroad was originally chartered in 1833 as the Andover and Wilmington R. R. and was completed between these towns and opened for operation, August 8, 1836. It then made a connection with the Boston and Lowell R. R. at Wilmington, that being the only railroad in that vicinity at the time. The Andover and Wilmington R. R. was extended to Bradford in 1837, to Exeter in 1840 and to a connection with the Portland, Saco and Portsmouth R. R. at South Berwick Junction in 1842. The lines in the several states through which the road passed were under different names and separate charters. These

UNION STATION, BOSTON.

roads were afterwards consolidated under the name of the Boston & Maine Railroad. The business still continued to be transferred to the Boston & Lowell R. R. at Wilmington for Boston and intermediate points. About the time that the road was completed to South Berwick Junction a charter was obtained to extend it to Boston independently of the Boston and Lowell R. R. the change in line being made at what is now called Wilmington Junction. The extension passed through the towns of Reading, Melrose and Malden and was opened for business to the Haymarket Square Station, Boston, July 1, 1845. The original passenger station in Boston was located on ground now occupied by the Union passenger station, but the charter compelled the railroad to build to Haymarket Square and they were obliged to do so, but would gladly have avoided that expense if possible to do so as the company was poor and could not get money easily, and the business was not enough to pay interest on money already expended.

Dover was opened up to railroad communication in 1841, and is now entered by the Western, Eastern and Northern Divisions of the great Boston and Maine system and is afforded with passenger and freight facilities befitting its immense and growing interests. The management of the road has ever been alive to the needs and demands of the city, and to this, in a great degree, can be credited the position in which the city now finds herself among the municipalities of this and the adjoining States. On the Western Division there are twenty-four passenger trains in and out of Dover daily, and twelve on the Eastern Division (Portsmouth and Dover Branch). Those on the latter stop at Folsom street and Sawyer's, both within the city limits, and at Dover Point and Cushing's before reaching Portsmouth, a distance of 10.88 miles. In 1847, an act was passed by the State of New Hampshire authorizing the construction of the Cocheco Railroad from Dover to Alton Bay. The road was opened to Farmington in 1848 and to Alton Bay in 1851. It was reorganized in 1862 under the name of Dover and Winnipiseogee

Railroad. An operating contract was entered into with the Boston & Maine Railroad in 1863 for a term of fifty years. The road was purchased by the Boston & Maine Railroad in 1892, and is now operated with the Lake Shore Branch of the Concord & Montreal road as the Dover & Lakeport Branch (Northern Division). This road has been the prime factor in opening up this delightful region to tourists and pleasure parties of which the number increases with each succeeding year. Two trains run daily each way between Dover and Lakeport and one to Alton Bay.

The present station was erected in 1874. It is built of brick and contains a comfortable and well-appointed waiting-room, toilet rooms, offices, news stand, and baggage room. A projecting roof protects passengers from the inclemency of the weather in boarding trains.

The freight house is conveniently located on Broadway about one mile east of the passenger station and is a two story brick building measuring 250 x 50 feet in dimensions. There are also a carpenter shop and round house and about thirty-five men are employed. The immense business transacted in the freight department is shown by the average monthly figures as follows: local and foreign freight forwarded 3,336,577 lbs.; local and foreign freight received, year ending June 30, 1898, 9,406,872 lbs. George F. Mathes is the general agent of the company at Dover; S. H. Bell, ticket agent; T. L. Berry, freight cashier; B. A. Dow, baggage master and C. H. Pemberton, assistant roadmaster.

The management of the road is constantly improving the rolling stock and equipment and making the main and and branch lines as perfect as modern science in railroad building will permit. During the present season there will be laid in all about 100 miles of new rail, 75 and 85 lb. pattern.

Passengers traveling over the lines of the Boston & Maine are carried to all points in the Lake and White Mountain regions and to St. John, Halifax and Montreal in elegantly appointed vestibuled drawing room and sleeping cars, without

BOSTON & MAINE STATION, DOVER.

BOSTON & MAINE FREIGHT DEPOT, DOVER.

change, and the accommodations provided are equal to those of any railroad in the world.

The company employs about 15,000 men, one thousand at the Union Station, Boston. The pay roll averages $8,600,000 yearly. It owns and operates 700 locomotives, 1,200 passenger cars and 13,000 freight cars. Six hundred regular trains are run daily in and out of the Union Station, carrying 100,000 passengers, 6,000 pieces—200 truck loads—of baggage, 22,000 lbs. of daily papers and 800 bicycles. The general officers located in Boston are as follows:—Lucius Tuttle, President; T. A. Mackinnon, 1st Vice-President and Gen. Mgr.; Wm. F. Berry, 2d Vice-Pres. and Gen. Traffic Mgr.; Frank Barr, Asst. Gen. Mgr.; A. Blanchard, Treasurer; H. E. Fisher, Asst. Treas.; Wm. J. Hobbs, Gen. Auditor; D. J. Flanders, Gen. Passenger and Ticket Agent; Geo. E. Sturtevant, Asst. G. P. & T. Agt.; F. E. Brown, Asst. G. P. & T. A., Concord, N. H.; Geo. W. Storer, Asst. Gen. Pass. & Tkt. Agt.; M. T. Donovan, Gen. Freight Agent; D. W. Sanborn, Gen. Superintendent; J. A. Farrington, Purchasing Agt; Henry Bartlett, Supt. Motive Power: Wm. Merritt, Supt. Western Division; J. W. Sanborn, Supt. Northern Division, Sanbornville, N. H.; W. T. Perkins, Supt. Eastern Division; W. G. Bean, Supt. Southern Division; C. E. Lee, Supt. Wor. Nash. & Port. Div., Nashua, N. H.; H. E. Chamberlin, Supt. Concord Div., Concord, N. H.; H. E. Folsom, Supt. Connecticut and Passumpsic Division, Lyndonville, Vt.; G. E. Cummings, Supt. White Mtns. Div., Woodsville, N. H.; H. E. Howard, Supt. Car Service; H. Bissell, Chief Engineer; O. W. Greeley, Gen. Baggage Agent; A. C. Varnum, New England Passenger Agent; A. P. Massey, Traveling Passenger Agent.

YORK HARBOR AND BEACH R. R.

A sketch of the Boston & Maine Railroad would not be complete without a reference to the York Harbor & Beach R. R. which has done so much to promote the comfort and convenience of the many thousands in this section who annually avail themselves of the opportunity to visit these delightful summer resorts, made possible by the enterprise of this road. Prior to the construction of the Eastern Railroad from Boston to Portsmouth and of the Portland, Saco and Portsmouth Railroad between Portsmouth and Portland, York was on the direct line of the " Eastern Stage Route " from Portland to Boston, which originally crossed York river from the point of land on which the Marshall House now stands and was called " Stage Neck." When the Boston & Maine Railroad was built through Wells and Kennebunk in 1872 and 1873, the old stage line was discontinued and a daily line established from Cape Neddick to Portsmouth. Early pilgrims to York well remember the conveniences of travel in those days.

In the autumn of 1882 a public meeting was held in York to discuss the question of better facilities for transportation, which the growing business of the town seemed to demand. A statement of the business of the town was prepared and John E. Staples, Edward S. Marshall, Henry E. Evans and John C. Stewart were chosen a committee to wait upon President E. B. Phillips of the Eastern R. R., present the statement and urge the advisability of that company extending a line from Portsmouth to York.

Subsequently efforts were made to induce the Boston & Maine Railroad company, which had obtained control of the Eastern, to aid in constructing the line. Hon. Frank Jones of Portsmouth, then a director of the Boston and Maine, became personally interested in the matter. He had subscribed to the stock of the road and through his influence Mr. H. Bissell, the chief engineer of the B. & M., was sent to examine the various routes which had been surveyed. After carefully examining them all he reported to Mr. Jones and the company upon the feasibility of each line.

October 22, 1886, the specifications were completed and bids asked for the construction of the line. The bids were to be opened Monday, November 1st. These specifications were for a narrow guage railroad from York Beach to a point on the line of the B. & M. about

BATHING AT YORK BEAOH.
Reached by the York Harbor & Beach R. R.

half a mile east of Kittery Depot, now Kittery Junction.

When Mr. Jones saw the prospect of a narrow guage road fast becoming a certainty he at once telegraphed the Directors to postpone all contracts until a conference could be had between the Directors of the two companies. This was done. A committee of the directors of the Y. H. & B. met a similar committee of the B. & M. and the result was an agreement that the Y. H. & B. R. R. Co. would give a right of way from Kittery Junction to the terminus of the road and take $50,000 of the stock. The B. & M. would furnish the balance of the money to complete the road and take the stock certificates— as bonds were to be issued— also furnish all rolling stock and equipments at actual cost, give the Y. H. & B. R. R. the free use of the main line from Kittery Junction to Portsmouth, together with all terminal facilities in Portsmouth until the Y. H. & B. stock should pay a dividend of five per cent. and construct a standard guage road.

The first contract was let December 6, 1886. Work was immediately begun. August 8, 1887, the first train was run to Long Beach. The next week it reached the terminus at York Beach. The entire cost was something over $300,000.

The road is eleven miles long and passes through some of the most beautiful and picturesque scenery in the world. Its route is along the seashore which it skirts at places to the water's edge. Twelve round trips are made between Portsmouth and York Beach daily, the fare being but forty cents for the round trip. During the summer season from 8,000 to 27,000 passengers are carried each month. The present managers of this road are Lucius Tuttle, President ; Samuel W. Junkins, Clerk ; W. F. Berry, Gen. Traffic Mgr. ; Amos Blanchard, Treasurer ; W. J. Hobbs, Auditor ; Dana J. Flanders, General Passenger and Ticket Agent ; M. T. Donovan, Gen. Freight Agent ; and Winslow T. Perkins, Superintendent.

George F. Mathes.

GEORGE F. MATHES, GENERAL AGENT B. & M.

George F. Mathes, general agent of the Boston & Maine Railroad at Dover, was born in Rochester in 1856, and received his education at the Rochester High School. Upon the completion of his studies he went railroading, obtaining employment with the old Portsmouth, Great Falls & Conway Railroad as brakeman, and was subsequently promoted to be baggagemaster. Always faithful in the performance of his duties it was not long before he was appointed conductor, in which capacity he served up to the time of receiving his present important and responsible position in May, 1893. Mr. Mathes has proven himself to be a man of excellent executive ability, and discharges the duties of his office in a manner that has won for him the confidence of the great company he so ably represents. He is also much esteemed by the traveling public who appreciate his unfailing courtesy and the despatch with which all business matters are attended to. Adding personal merit to the influence of place, he may well be accorded a position among our representative business men.

In 1889 Mr. Mathes was elected a member of the Constitutional Convention which assembled at Concord. Four years later he represented Wolfboro in the legislature, serving on various committees, and displaying considerable ability which won him high praise from his constituents. Mr. Mathes married in 1874, Fanny A. Parker, daughter of the late Charles H. Parker, editor

W. F. CARTLAND.

of the Granite State News, and has one son, Charles A. Mathes, now twenty-two years of age and a young man of much promise. Mr. Mathes has a pleasant home at 26 Sixth street and has a large and ever increasing circle of friends.

William F. Cartland.

The number of men who succeed in life, although they start in without or almost without any capital is really wonderful and must be primarily ascribed to a wonderful determination to overcome the numerous obstacles which impede the pathway to prosperity. A notable example of a self made man whose energy, perseverance and sound judgment have placed him in the front rank of successful business men, is William F. Cartland, the subject of this sketch.

Mr. Cartland was born in Parsonfield, Me., January 5, 1860, and acquired his education at the district school. Upon leaving school he worked on his father's farm, his arduous labors eminently fitting him for the many vicissitudes which are to be encountered by the young man beginning life with only an indomitable will power and an active brain as his capital. At eighteen years of age he came to Dover and entered the employment of his uncle, William P. Tuttle, where he remained for three years when he entered the employ of J. Frank Roberts and devoted himself assiduously to learning the grocery business. From Mr. Roberts' he went to work for W. S. Wiggin, but the spirit of enterprise which is one of his characteristics was strong within him and his ambition led him to seek broader fields of usefulness than come within the scope of a grocery clerk. He yearned to have a business of his own where he could develop his latent powers and it was not long before the opportunity presented itself. In 1885 Mr. Cartland bought out Mr. John Kimball, of the firm of Kimball & Tasker, which was then located in the

Freeman Block where now stands the Strafford Bank building. The firm of Tasker & Cartland was formed July 1, 1885, and continued until January 1, 1898, when Mr. Cartland became sole proprietor of the great business which had been built up by the perseverance and energy of the firm. In 1892 the business was moved from the Freeman Block to a portion of the present premises, but the growing demands made upon the resources of the firm speedily compelled them to secure larger premises with the result that two years later the adjoining

lighted by electricity. The exceptionally heavy stock carried, which is the largest in southern New Hampshire, embraces a complete assortment of fine groceries and foreign delicacies of every description, and a specialty is made of family flours, coffee, tea and canned goods of the choicest brands. None but strictly first class goods are kept in the store, everything is guaranteed to be exactly as represented, and the prices which obtain are uniformly reasonable. Mr. Cartland being a large cash purchaser is enabled to undersell others who deal in smaller quantities and offers

RESIDENCE OF W. F. CARTLAND.

store was added, making this the largest grocery store in the city. The largely increased volume of trade which has resulted from these increased facilities has proven how sound was the judgment which prompted the move. The premises are located at 41-43 Locust street on which they have a frontage of forty feet, the floor space occupying 3200 square feet, with basement, making a total of 6400 square feet, with a large storehouse on Washington street. It is neatly fitted up and excellently arranged throughout, fitted with handsome plate glass windows and

to his customers the benefit of the discounts obtained by his wholesale transactions. Ten courteous assistants attend to the requirements of customers and four delivery teams are in active service delivering goods. Mr. Cartland's business has steadily increased until it has become the largest of its kind in the city of Dover. The trade of the house extends not only throughout the city limits but reaches out to Rochester, Somersworth, Exeter, Newmarket and Berwick, Me. The purchasing and distribution of the stock show that it is selected with the care character-

INTERIOR VIEW OF GROCERY STORE OF W. F. CARTLAND.

INTERIOR VIEW OF GROCERY STORE OF W. F. CARTLAND.

istic of a prudent, wide awake and thorough business man, catering for a strictly first class trade and anxious to meet the demands of his patrons.

Mr. Cartland is a good type of the self made man, who rises by his own exertions from a moderate beginning to a foremost place in his particular trade. He has a handsome residence on Highland street, surrounded by tastefully laid out grounds and is looked upon as one of Dover's ablest and most successful business men.

George D. Barrett.

The steady growth of Dover has rendered active the operations in real estate, and the development of the in-

GEORGE D. BARRETT.

and conducts the largest fire insurance business in the city, representing fifteen of the largest American and English companies, whose combined assets are over $50,000,000. He makes a specialty of the general management of estates, taking the entire charge, securing responsible tenants, effecting repairs, and in every way maintaining the property up to the highest productive standard. Mr. Barrett has always upon his books the best available bargains in lands, houses, stores, etc. He also effects exchanges of real estate, secures loans to any amount on bond or mortgage security, and sells administrators, executors and all kinds of surety bonds

G. D. BARRETT'S OFFICE.

dustries of the city are constantly increasing the value of property and making its possession most valuable. Mr. Barrett is the acknowledged leading real estate agent at a very small cost. The extent of his business and his splendid facilities enable him to meet all demands made upon his resources in a thoroughly satisfactory manner. Mr. Barrett was born at Edmeston, N. Y., December 4, 1864, and was educated at Colgate University. He engaged in the insurance business in Rome, N. Y., for some years, coming to Dover in July, 1894. His office is located in the Masonic Temple. During his residence in Dover he has proved himself a thoroughly public-spirited citizen, and has always given a hearty support to every measure best calculated to advance the city's interests. Mr. Barrett is secretary of the Dover Co-operative bank and of the Dover Commercial club, and works diligently to promote the welfare of both organizations.

rooms for guests are provided with all the improvements of modern hotel life, including electric call bells, gas and electric lights and steam heat.

The American was opened in June, 1867, by Peirce and True, the present partnership of A. T. Peirce and Thomas K. Cushman being formed ten years later. Both the partners have had an extended experience in the hotel business and know how to minister to the requirements of their guests so as to insure their comfort.

Col. Adams T. Peirce, who was chairman of the legislative Committee on County Affairs and a member of the Committee on National Affairs, was born in 1844 at

THE AMERICAN.

The American.

The American under the direction of A. T. Peirce & Co. is one of the best known hotels in this section. Situated on Central avenue, facing Franklin square, in the commercial centre of the city and within two minutes walk of the B. & M. station, its location is singularly convenient for the requirements of the traveling public. The building is a handsome three and a half story brick structure, originally erected as a private residence and since considerably enlarged by its present proprietors. It is furnished and decorated throughout in a tasteful manner and the

North Yarmouth, Me., receiving his education at the South Paris Academy. He is chairman of the Republican City Committee and ex-president of the Dover Commercial Club, a member of the Amoskeag Veterans, Manchester, and of the Ancient and Honorable Artillery Company, Boston. Colonel Peirce served as U. S. Marshal from the district of New Hampshire from 1890 to 1894. He was a member of the staff of the late Governor Weston, with the rank of Colonel. He is a member of several secret orders, among them Mt. Pleasant Lodge I. O. O. F., Wanalanset Tribe of Red Men and has been commander of Canton Parker No. 3, P. M.

Thomas K. Cushman is a native of New Gloucester, Me., and received his education at the High school there. Upon leaving school he learned the trade of carriage maker at New Haven, Conn., which he followed until 1862 when he enlisted in the Fifteenth Connecticut Infantry from which he was transferred to the Eighth Conn. Regiment and saw service at Fredericksburg, Peters-

Colonel Daniel Hall.

Daniel Hall was born in Barrington, February 28, 1832. His first known American ancestor was John Hall, who appears to have come to Dover in 1649 with his brother Ralph from Charlestown, Mass. Mr. Daniel Hall's life as a boy was on the farm. He attended the district school and when about sixteen years

COLONEL DANIEL HALL.

burg and Richmond. Upon leaving the army he went to the Tontine House, Brunswick, Me., then kept by Colonel Peirce and subsequently spent two years at the Kimball House, Atlanta, Ga. He left the Kimball House to enter into partnership with Colonel Peirce at Claremont and from thence came to Dover in 1877 to form the present partnership.

of age secured two terms in the Strafford academy. In 1849 he spent one term at the New Hampshire Conference Seminary, Northfield, N. H., after which he prepared himself for Dartmouth College, which he entered in 1850. In 1854 he graduated at the head of his class and was valedictorian.

In the fall of 1854 he was appointed a clerk in the New York Custom House and held this position until March, 1858, when he was removed from office on account of his marked antipathy to the Kansas-Nebraska bill. While in New York he entered upon the study of the law and continued his studies, upon returning to Dover, in the office of the late Hon. Daniel M. Christie, being admitted to the bar in the May term, 1860. He opened an office at Dover and commenced practice.

In 1859 he was appointed by the Governor and Council School Commissioner for Strafford County and re-appointed in 1860. He was appointed secretary of the United States Committee to investi-

himself, but in 1863 his health suffered and he was forced to leave the front in December, 1863. In June, 1864, he was appointed provost-marshal of the First New Hampshire District at Portsmouth where he remained until the close of the war, when he resumed the practice of law in Dover. He was appointed clerk of the Supreme Court of Strafford County in 1866 and Judge of the Police Court in 1868, an office he acceptably filled until 1874. In the meantime he had been Judge Advocate with the rank of major in the military of New Hampshire under Governor Smythe and held a position on

RESIDENCE OF COLONEL DANIEL HALL.

gate the surrender of the Norfolk Navy Yard in 1861. Afterwards he was appointed clerk of the Senate Committee on Naval Affairs at Washington in which capacity he served until March, 1862, when he was commissioned aide-de-camp and captain in the regular army. He was assigned to duty with General John C. Fremont who, however, retired from his command, and Captain Hall was transferred to the staff of General A. W. Whipple. During his service Captain Hall participated in the battles of Antietam, Fredericksburg, Chancellorsville, Gettysburg, and others, winning distinction for

the staff of Governor Harriman which gave him his usual title of Colonel. Colonel Hall was president of the Republican State Convention at Concord in 1873. He had been for some years a member of the Republican State Committee, when in 1873 he was selected as chairman of that committee continuing so until 1877. He was also chairman of the New Hampshire delegation to the Republican National Convention at Cincinnati in 1876, and in 1876-77 was, by appointment of Governor Cheney, reporter of the decisions of the Supreme Court of New Hampshire. In 1877 he succeeded Governor Harriman as naval officer at the port of Boston, an office co-ordinate with that of collector, and was upon the expiration of his term re-appointed by President Arthur for a further term of four years. He is at present a director of the Strafford National bank, trustee of the Strafford Savings bank and trustee of the Dover Public Library, and has ever used his great influence to advance the interests and prosperity of the city. Colonel Hall has manifested a deep interest in the Grand Army of the Republic, passing through all its chairs. He was Department Commander of New Hampshire in 1892 and is a member of the Massachusetts Order of the Loyal Legion of the United States. Colonel Hall married January 25, 1877, Sophia, daughter of Jonathan T. and Sarah (Hanson) Dodge of Rochester and has one son, Arthur Wellesley Hall, born August 30, 1878. The beautiful residence erected by him at the corner of Summer and Belknap streets and adorned with cultivated taste, has not its least charm in a splendid library of carefully selected literature.

Public addresses have, as occasions demanded, exhibited the thoughtful political student, a patriotic love of country, and the ripeness of the accomplished scholar. Some permanent evidence of his power as a scholar and orator may be found in a volume published by him in 1892, entitled " Occasional Addresses," and containing addresses on Abraham Lincoln, Ulysses S. Grant, Daniel M. Christie, John P. Hale, John B. Gough, Governor Edward F. Noyes, and other topics.

Fidelity to every engagement, good faith to every principle espoused, firmness in determination, great industry and usefulness in every work undertaken have insured him success.

Colonel Hall enjoys the admiration of his fellow citizens at large for unusual gifts as a scholar and public speaker, while the strength and sincerity of his political convictions, the influence he has uniformly exerted for the triumph of policies which he deems essential for the good of the state and nation, and his integrity in public and private life, entitle him, in the opinion of his numerous friends, to higher honors than any he has received.

Hon. J. W. Jewell.

Hon. John Woodman Jewell, General Agent of the Massachusetts Mutual Life Insurance Company of Springfield, Mass., was born in Strafford, N. H., July 26, 1831. In early life he learned to labor, being put at work in his father's tanyard and currying shop where he mastered all its details, but not liking the business, at the age of eighteen, with his father's consent, he hired out on a farm—not being physically strong, in a short time was taken sick with hemorrhages of the stomach and was obliged to remain quiet for a long time. After his recovery, having had but limited school privileges, averaging not more than six weeks a year in the town schools, he entered Strafford Seminary (now Austin Academy) and afterwards attended Gilmanton Academy for several terms, teaching school winters. In 1853 he entered a store in Newmarket as clerk where he remained about a year when he returned to his native town and entered the employ of the late Hon. Benning W. Jenness as clerk in his store with whom he remained for ten years, until Mr. Jenness removed to Cleveland, Ohio, when he succeeded him in business. He was successful, did a large business and was the leading business man of the town for thirty years. In politics he was a Democrat and took an active part in all political questions, and was frequently honored by his townsmen with different offices in their gift, serving as moderator, superintendent of schools, selectman, and representative in the legislature, and was postmaster for ten years. He was sheriff of Strafford County for two years, from 1874 to 1876, and a member of the Governor's Council two years, from 1885 to 1887, serving on the State Prison Committee, committee to audit the State Treasurer's accounts and committee to look after the expenditures of the money appropriated by the state for repairs of the highways in the northern part of the state. In 1891 Mr. Jewell came to Dover and took charge of the business of the Massachusetts Mutual Life Insurance Company as agent and

HON. JOHN WOODMAN JEWELL.

RESIDENCE OF HON. J. W. JEWELL, COR. HAM AND EAST CONCORD STREETS.

in January, 1892, he was appointed General Agent of the company. His office is at 32 Masonic Temple. In the life insurance business he has been quite as successful as he was in mercantile affairs. By earnest, honest effort he has built up a very lucrative business. In 1853 Mr. Jewell married Miss Sarah Folsom Gale of Upper Gilmanton (now Belmont). By this union three children were born to them, one son and two daughters. The

and Maria (Goodhue) Trickey, was born in Brookfield, Carroll County, August 14, 1833. His mother was a descendant of Governor Thomas Wiggin and is now living with Mrs. Trickey and in full possession of all her faculties, although ninety-three years of age. Mr. Trickey received his education at the district school and the academy at Wakefield, and at the age of seventeen taught school at New Durham where he received five dollars a month more than

THE LATE CHARLES HENRY TRICKEY.

son, a bright, active and popular business man, who was associated with his father in business at Strafford under the firm name of J. W. Jewell & Son, died in 1893. One daughter lives at home, the other is married and resides in Manchester.

The Late Charles Henry Trickey.

Charles Henry Trickey, son of Lemuel

any other teacher on account of his successful methods in imparting instruction to his pupils. In 1853 he came to Dover as clerk to John E. Bickford, merchant tailor, subsequently becoming a partner and finally buying out the business which he successfully conducted until 1870 when he sold it. Mr. Trickey then bought out the coal, wood and lumber business of M. D. Page and also secured an interest in

the teaming and hay enterprise of G. W.
Avery, in which he remained until his demise February 2, 1896. In his business
dealings he was singularly successful, owing largely to his close personal attention
and the foresight he displayed. During
his lifetime the sales of coal increased
from 600 to over 10,000 tons per annum.
He had a keen, quick perception of business, an intuitive knowledge of cause and
effect and a steady determination to do
exactly as he agreed, keeping his word in

through Mr. Trickey's influence and at his
suggestion that the river channel was
straightened and deepened by the government, which resulted in a considerable increase in the tonnage entering the port.
In politics Mr. Trickey was an ardent Republican. Quiet and unostentatious, he
shrank from political honors and prefer-
ment, neither caring for nor seeking office,
although frequently urged to do so by his
friends. In private life he was characterized by modest and unassuming ways and

THE STRAFFORD BANKS BUILDING.

all matters pertaining to business. Mr.
Trickey did not remain an idle spectator
of events but largely interested himself in
all matters concerning the improvement
and development of the community. He
worked zealously for the public welfare
and many important public improvements
were instigated by him. He was one of
the charter members and a director of
the Dover Navigation Co., and one of
their vessels was named for him. It was

a great attachment to home and the home
circle. He was married Dec. 25, 1869,
to Ada, daughter of ex-Mayor Albert
Bond, and had two children, Marion Gertrude, married to Rev. George A. Alcott,
and Lola Maude, now a teacher in Connecticut. Mr. Trickey was again married
April 28, 1886, to Georgietta Hanson, two
children of this marriage surviving him,
Charles Lemuel and Mabel Grace. Upon
Mr. Trickey's demise his widow under-

took the conduct of the large business of her late husband and has since capably managed it.

The Strafford National Bank.

The first bank in Dover was incorporated by the Legislature, by an act approved June 11, 1803, under the name of "The President, Directors, and Company of the New Hampshire Strafford Bank," the charter being for twenty years. A new act extending its charter was accepted July 1, 1822.

John Currier, Moses Paul, Ezekiel Hurd, Nathaniel Young, and Eleazer Davis Chamberlain. William Woodman, president; Asa A. Tufts, cashier.

On July 1, 1865, the Strafford Bank surrendered its state charter and accepted a charter from the United States, under the name of the Strafford National Bank, the old officers being re-chosen to the same offices in the new bank. The capital at that time was $150,000, but has since been increased to $200,000. There is at present a surplus of $120,000 and the deposits average $500,000.

INTERIOR STRAFFORD NATIONAL BANK.

The Strafford Bank was incorporated by an act passed July 9, 1846, to continue to June 1, 1867. The incorporators were Daniel Osborne, William Hale, John H. Wheeler, Daniel M. Christie, Nathaniel Young, George Andrews, William Hale, Jr., Moses Paul, John Currier, Joseph Morrill, Jeremy Perkins, and William Woodman. They organized October 17, 1846, to commence business January 4, 1847, the capital to be $100,000, which was increased to $120,000 by vote July 7, 1857. The first board of directors were William Woodman, Daniel M. Christie,

This bank now occupies the beautiful building erected by it in connection with Strafford Savings Bank in 1895. It stands on the corner of Washington street and Central avenue and is one of the city's most notable architectural features.

Woodbury & Leighton of Boston were the builders and Mr. A. T. Ramsdell of Dover the architect. The structure is of Milford pink granite, four stories in height and having a frontage of 115 feet on Washington street. The offices occupied by the bank are handsomely furnished and finished in quartered oak and mahogany, commodious and well lighted. A prettier bank office could not be desired. It is fitted up in the most modern design, and with all conveniences for the dispatch of business. In the rear of the banking-room is a large and handsomely furnished directors' and president's room and a small room for the use of depositors and customers. The safety deposit vaults are large and are marvels of strength and safety, embodying all the latest devices known to modern scientific safe building.

From the hour when its doors were first opened for business to the present, the

wrecked less wisely directed institutions. The Strafford bank enjoys unsurpassed facilities for the transaction of general banking in all its branches—the care of deposits, discounts of reliable paper, the issue of drafts and letters of credit on all American and foreign monetary centres, the making and forwarding of collections, etc. Especial attention is given to individual, firm and corporation accounts, and to the collection of dividends of all kinds, which service is performed for depositors free of charge.

The officers and board of directors em-

INTERIOR STRAFFORD SAVINGS BANK.

course of this institution has been one of the most careful and conservative management, combined with a liberal policy toward all responsibly conducted, legitimate enterprises in behalf of which its aid has been invoked. Nothing of a doubtful or risky character has ever received the sanction of its officers or directors, and, as a consequence, the Strafford Bank, both before and since its enrollment among the national banks, has ever borne the deserved reputation of absolute reliability— a fortress of finance unaffected by the storms which from time to time have

brace such well known and responsible citizens as Elisha R. Brown, President; Directors, Ex-Governor Charles H. Sawyer, Colonel Samuel C. Fisher, Judge George S. Frost, James W. Bartlett, Charles S. Cartland, and Colonel Daniel Hall; Cashier, Charles S. Cartland.

The Strafford Savings Bank.

On the 27th of June, 1823, a charter was granted for incorporation of the Savings Bank for the County of Strafford, the fifth savings bank in the United States, and January 31, 1824, a meeting of the corporators was held at the old Court House, Tuttle square, to accept the charter. On February 7th, John Wheeler was chosen President and its Vice-Presidents were John Williams and Stephen Hanson, with John W. Mellen, Clerk. Its Trustees were Jesse Varney, James Bartlett, Joseph Smith, Jacob Kettredge, John B. Odiorne, Wm. Flagg, Barnabas H. Palmer, Wm. Woodman, George Piper, Joseph W. Clary, Moses Paul, and Wm. Palmer.

The bank was first located in the brick building on Central avenue now owned by Dr. John R. Ham. At first it was open for business on Friday afternoon of each week from 3 to 6 o'clock. The first deposit was made by Stephen Hanson for his son, Wm. R. Hanson, on Feb. 28, 1824.

In 1846 the Strafford Bank erected a bank building on Washington street (its present location) and in 1847 the Savings Bank moved into rooms on the same floor of said block, with separate vault facilities. The growth of business during the next decade was such that more room was needed, and the entire second story was fitted up and there the bank continued until July, 1895, when they were temporarily located in the Cocheco Corporation next to their counting rooms, while the old bank building was removed and the new block now known as Strafford Banks Building was erected by this bank in connection with Strafford National Bank, and in which fine, commodious quarters were made for the increasing needs of such an institution, and occupied by it in July, 1896. Its corporate name was changed by act of Legislature in June, 1891, to Strafford Savings Bank.

In 1849, 25 years after its books were open for business, its deposits were $400,-461, with 2500 depositors.

In 1874, at completion of its half century, the deposits were $2,088,369, number of depositors 4963.

In 1898 the number of depositors is 9700, and amount to credit of said accounts is $5,000,000, with a guaranty fund of $300,000.

This remarkable growth of the Savings Bank had back of it something more than the generally prosperous condition of the section it drew upon, and that important something was the confidence in its methods and condition that had been established by its years of careful and conservative management. Its officers have, from the beginning, been men of this class. Its trustees and boards of investment, its presidents and treasurers have been persons who earned and commanded public confidence. From its inception until now it is truthfully claimed for the Strafford Savings Bank that there is no provision the state has made for the safety and advantage of savings bank depositors that this bank has not willingly, zealously and to the utmost of its ability applied and carried out. And it has had its reward in the ever increasing volume of its deposits which now reach the sum of $5,000,000.

The present officers of the bank are Elisha R. Brown, President ; Ex-Governor Charles H. Sawyer, First Vice President ; Colonel Samuel C. Fisher, Second Vice President ; Trustees, Elisha R. Brown, Ex-Governor Charles H. Sawyer, Colonel Samuel C. Fisher, John Holland, John H. Hurd, Hon. B. Frank Nealley, Colonel Daniel Hall, and A. G. Whittemore, Esq. ; Executive Officer, Elisha R. Brown ; Treasurer and Secretary, Albert O. Mathes.

The First (Congregational) Church.

This is the fifth and present house of worship of the First Church in Dover. Two hundred and sixty-five years ago, in October, 1633, Rev. William Leverich, a graduate of Emmanuel College, Cambridge, England, began preaching in the settlement at Hilton's Point on Dover Neck, and the First Parish may be said to date from that event. During his ministry of about two years, the first meeting-house was erected. In December, 1638, Rev. Hanserd Knollys, the third minister of the First Parish, organized the First Church. A generation later, the second meeting-house was erected on the well known site where are to be seen at the present time remnants of the ancient fortification. During more than half a century the church worshipped in that fortified meeting-house; then, moving still further north, made its third home, during almost another half century, on Pine Hill. The fourth house of worship stood upon the site of the present one, and opened its doors to the congregation in 1758. The present meeting-house was dedicated December 31, 1829, and a half century later, after undergoing a radical reconstruction at an expense of about twenty-three thousand dollars, was rededicated on Thanksgiving evening, November 28, 1878. A large and convenient chapel, connecting with the church in the rear, and costing over thirteen thousand dollars, was dedicated in April 1889. This ancient church, the oldest in New Hampshire, stands for spiritual life, and liberty, and progress, for all that is true and good. In patriotic devotion its influence has been marked

since the days when Jeremy Belknap did so much to inspire and guide the Revolution. In missionary zeal and work this church takes a leading position. One of its honored pastors said on the occasion of the two hundred and fiftieth anniversary of the First Parish, "The church so feebly born has strengthened its stakes and enlarged its borders, untouched by time, asserting itself with an ever-clearer utterance in the community and state, more vigorous and strong in every last

stage of its growth, and, like the tree planted by the ever-running waters, 'bringing forth fruit in old age.' But its prolific life has not been kept within itself. This church has been rightly called a 'mother church.' She has established from her membership nearly every Congregational church in this vicinity, and strengthened from it almost every Congregational church in the state. And more than this, she has sent forth from her inexhaustible loins children who have built up, even in her very presence, churches of other orders."

REV. GEORGE E. HALL, D. D.

George Edward Hall, D. D., pastor of the First church in Dover, was born in Jamaica, West Indies, February 23, 1851, son of the Reverend Heman B. and Sophronia (Brooks) Hall. In the paternal line he traces his descent from John Hall of Medford,

THE FIRST CONGREGATIONAL CHURCH.

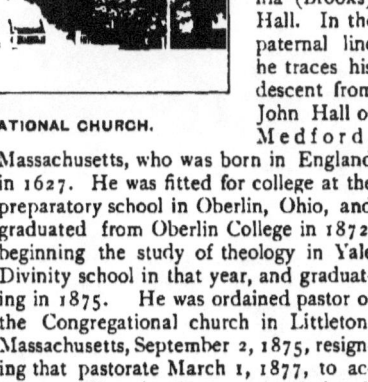

Massachusetts, who was born in England in 1627. He was fitted for college at the preparatory school in Oberlin, Ohio, and graduated from Oberlin College in 1872, beginning the study of theology in Yale Divinity school in that year, and graduating in 1875. He was ordained pastor of the Congregational church in Littleton, Massachusetts, September 2, 1875, resigning that pastorate March 1, 1877, to accept a call to the Congregational church in Vergennes, Vermont, where he was installed May 2, 1877. His pastorate in Vergennes was highly successful, but he resigned in October, 1883, to accept a call to Dover, and was installed over the First church on January 2, 1884. Dr. Hall is the twenty-third on the roll of pastors of this historical church. His pastorate of more than fourteen years, continuing with unabated strength, has been very successful and happy. In January of 1895, the church voted Dr. Hall six months' vacation to visit Egypt and the Holy Land, and a further manifestation of regard was a testimonial by voluntary gifts of eight hundred dollars, presented to him on the eve of his departure. Mr. Hall has been five times a member of the National Council (Triennial) of Congregational churches. He is a Trustee and one of the Executive Committee of the New Hampshire Home Missionary Society.

REV. GEORGE E. HALL, D. D.

He is a corporate member of the American Board of Commissioners for Foreign Missions. He received the degree of Doctor of Divinity from Dartmouth College in 1893. He is a member of the School Committee of Dover. He has been for five years chaplain of the First Regiment New Hampshire National Guard. He holds membership in the Winthrop club of Boston and the Monday

club of Boston. Mr. Hall was married June 20, 1877, to Alice Monroe, daughter of the late James Monroe Peabody of Lowell, Massachusetts. Mrs. Hall died April 6, 1883, leaving two children, Alice Miriam and Henry Monroe. Mr. Hall married April 16, 1890, Elizabeth Kneeland, daughter of the late William McFarland of Salem, Massachusetts, whose father was the Rev. Asa McFarland, D. D., of Concord. They have two children, John McFarland and George William Hall.

St. John's Methodist Episcopal Church.

From the establishment of the " First Church " in 1638 no other church existed in Dover though there was " Society" of Friends, till the introduction of Methodism. In 1819, the first Methodist meetings for worship were held at a small village which then existed some two miles up the river from the present city proper, called the Upper Factory, where was located a small manufacturing establishment. Rev. John Lord, afterward a prominent minister in Maine, then traveling on the Rochester Circuit, visited this village in 1819 and preached to the people and organized a " class " and a Sunday school. The late venerable Solomon Gray and the late George W. Wendell of Somersworth, then resided at the Upper Factory and were pioneers of Methodism in Dover.

From this beginning in 1819 to 1823 when Dover was made a separate charge the records are very meagre. The first preaching at the village was in the old Court House. Rev. Jotham Horton was the first regularly stationed preacher at Dover.

As the work grew, it became evident that better accommodations were needed, and measures were taken in 1824,—Mr. Horton's second year, —for the erection of a house of worship. A lot of land (that on which the present house stands), was procured of the heirs of the celebrated Major Richard Waldron, whose grave is in the immediate vicinity. The committee appointed to conduct the building enterprise were among the most substantial citizens. They were Dr. Joseph Smith, Robert Rogers, George Piper, William Palmer, Jeremy, H. Titcomb, Lewis B. Tibbetts, and Rev. Jotham Horton, the pastor. The first Board of Trustees were Joseph Smith,

REV. DR. BABCOCK.

Lewis B. Tibbetts, Barnabus H. Palmer, Richard Walker, George Piper, Geo. W. Edgerly, and Theodore Littlefield. No one of these is now living. This church answered its purpose very well till when in 1828 an addition was built on the rear end, of sixteen and one-half feet. This church has always been a vigorous body, and has been served by some of the ablest ministers of the denomination. The present church edifice was erected on the site of the original one, in 1875. It cost without the lot about $40,000. That includes the organ and the chime of nine bells. Its seating capacity is about one thousand.

From the beginning this church has always maintained a vigorous Sunday school. The present pastor is Rev. D. C. Babcock, D.D.

REV. D. C. BABCOCK, D.D.

Rev. Daniel Clark Babcock, D. D., was born in Blandford, Mass., May 31st, 1835. His father, Russell Babcock, and his mother, Susan A. (Clark) were natives of So. Kingston, R. I. He was the second of four sons, but

ST. JOHN'S METHODIST EPISCOPAL CHURCH.

is now the only member of the family living. His mother died when he was nine years of age and his father before he was twenty. The youngest brother died in infancy. The oldest was lost at sea when a young man, and the other died in Philadelphia, Pa., in 1887.

Mr. B. took his academic training in the East Douglas, Mass., High School, at the Providence Conference Seminary, East Greenwich, R. I., and at the Vermont Conference Seminary, then at Newbury, now at Montpelier. He graduated from the school of theology of the Boston University, then at Concord, N. H., in June, 1864. The Honorary Degree—Doctor of Divinity, was conferred by the American Temperance University in 1896.

Mr. B. joined the New Hampshire Conference of the Methodist Episcopal church in April, 1861, having served four years prior to that as a "Local Preacher." He served as pastor in the following order, at Bow, Fisherville, now Penacook, Salem Depot, High Street, Great Falls, now Somersworth, Claremont, St. Paul's, Manchester, and Chestnut St., Nashua. While at Nashua he was G. C. T. of the Good Templars of New Hampshire.

As the result of over work he found rest a necessity, and took a nominal appointment after one year at Nashua, spending much of the year in traveling.

During that year he was elected Corresponding Secretary of the Pennsylvania Temperance Union, and entered that field in March, 1872, with headquarters in Philadelphia. He served in that capacity until May, 1888. During the last eight years of that period he was also District Secretary of the National Temperance Society and Publication House.

Mr. B. returned to pastoral work in the spring of 1888, and has served at Claremont, Lancaster and Whitefield. In April, 1896, he consented to give a year to the field work of the Law and Order League of New Hampshire, of which he is Sec-Treas. He was appointed pastor of St. John's church, Dover, in April, 1897, by Bishop W. X. Ninde, and for a second year in April, 1898, by Bishop W. F. Mallalieu.

He united in marriage with Miss Clara A. Parkman of Sutton, Mass., in April, 1860. They have two daughters, Miss Susie Parkman, who is with them, and Mrs. Mary A., wife of Rev. J. Roy Dinsmore, pastor at North Haverhill, N. H.

PIERCE MEMORIAL CHURCH (UNIVERSALIST).

Peirce Memorial Church.
(UNIVERSALIST).

The Universalist Church, known as the Peirce Memorial, on Central avenue, was organized in 1837.

There was preaching of Universalism in Dover some years previous to that date. At first the society worshipped in a hall.

About 1838 a church edifice was built by the society on Third street. The building was enlarged in 1847.

This was the place of worship until about 1880 when the church was sold for business purposes. In 1883 the present substantial and beautiful brick edifice was dedicated. The building, costing $30,000, was the gift of Thomas W. Peirce in memory of his parents.

Since the present society was reorganized in 1883, these pastors have been settled. Rev. S. H. McCollester, D. D., Rev. Walter Scott Vail, Rev. Fred W. Dillingham, Rev. Royal T. Sawyer, and Rev. Ezra Almon Hoyt the present pastor, who began his work in this city in 1891.

REV. E. A. HOYT.

Rev. Ezra Almon Hoyt, pastor of Peirce Memorial Church, was born in Hanover, Maine, October 31, 1855. His boyhood and youth were spent on a farm. His early education was in the district school. When eighteen years old he went to the village school for the first time. From that time his real education dated. Teaching school in winter he earned money to attend Hebron Academy and

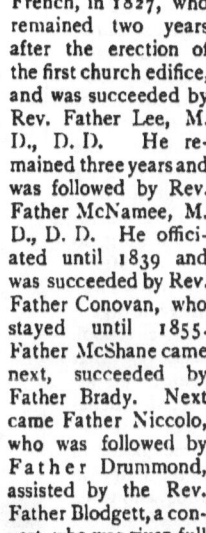

REV. E. A. HOYT.

Westbrook Seminary, from which he graduated in 1878. In the fall of that year he entered Tufts College, graduating with class of '82. He was ordained to the ministry at Thompsonville, Conn. His pastorates since ordination have been in Skowhegan, Maine, St. Johnsbury, Vermont, and his present pastorate in Dover, which began in 1891.

St. Mary's Roman Catholic Church.

Mass was first said in Dover in the winter of 1826 by Rev. Virgil H. Barber,

S. J. Among the prominent pioneer Catholics in Dover were William Ashcroft, John Burns, Francis G. O'Neill, Philip F. Scanlan, and Wm. McDevitt.

Services were first held in the Court House. May 17, 1828, the corner stone of the first Catholic church was laid and was completed and accepted in June, 1829. It cost $2800. The church was consecrated September 26, 1830, by Rt. Rev. Dr. Dominick Fenwick of Boston. The rapid growth of the church demanded a more commodious edifice and in 1872 the present building was completed.

The first regular pastor of the church was Rev. Father French, in 1827, who remained two years after the erection of the first church edifice, and was succeeded by Rev. Father Lee, M. D., D. D. He remained three years and was followed by Rev. Father McNamee, M. D., D. D. He officiated until 1839 and was succeeded by Rev. Father Conovan, who stayed until 1855. Father McShane came next, succeeded by Father Brady. Next came Father Niccolo, who was followed by Father Drummond, assisted by the Rev. Father Blodgett, a convert, who was given full charge of the parish before he had been here a year, on account of the feebleness of Father Drummond.

Father Blodgett was one of the most able and enterprising priests that ever presided over this parish. It was through him that the New Hampshire House property and the new Catholic cemetery were secured, and had he lived, he would have erected upon this property one of the finest churches in the State. Father Blodgett died May 15, 1881, and was the first priest to be buried in Dover. Rev. Father Murphy succeeded and was soon given the entire charge of the parish.

REV. DANIEL W. MURPHY.

Father Murphy assumed the charge of St. Mary's parish in 1881. He was born in Liscarroll, Ireland, Nov. 24, 1838, studied at the classical school of Charleville and at the college of Middleton, and took his philosophical and part of his theological courses at All Hallows, finishing his studies for the priesthood in the Grand Seminary of Montreal. He was ordained in Portland, Aug. 21, 1861, by Bishop Bacon. After serving a short time as assistant at the Portland cathedral, he was made pastor of Houlton, Maine, at the end of 1861 coming to take temporary charge of Dover in 1862, and returning to Houlton after a few months, where he organized a school. While in that charge, he attended Benedicta. He became pastor of Bath, Maine, in 1864, and while there built a new rectory, and established a school. In October, 1865, he was transferred to Portsmouth. He went to Keene in 1869, to which parish twenty-one out-missions were then attached. He built a rectory and remodeled the church in Keene, built churches at Peterboro and Ashuelot, bought the Episcopal church in Walpole, and instituted church-building funds in Claremont and Charlestown. In 1877, he was appointed pastor of Augusta, Maine, and while there enlarged the Augusta church and built a church in Hallowell.

From Augusta he removed to Dover.

In the September of his first year here Father Murphy began erecting, on the lot purchased by Father Blodgett, the Sacred Heart School (for girls), opening it in 1883, under a community of the Sisters of Mercy from Manchester, and remodeling for convent uses the large building which stood on the property ; and, during the latter year, he also virtually rebuilt the rectory, adding the present front, deepening the building by thirty-five feet, and putting on a Mansard roof, the expense of the improvement being $6,000. In 1884 he frescoed the church, furnished it with new gas fixtures and steam heating apparatus, and erected three new altars. Three years later, he purchased an estate on Court street, converting the house which stood thereon into an orphanage ; in 1888, he built St. Joseph's School (for boys) on Central avenue putting it at first in charge of the Sisters of Mercy ; during the following year he secured as teachers of the boys a band of Christian Brothers ; and in 1890 he erected a fine residence for the Brothers, and put stained-glass windows into the church. In 1891, he built the church tower, hanging therein a fine bell. In 1892, the county authorities entrusted to Father Murphy's care all the little Catholic girls of the county farm ; and he was obliged, consequently, to enlarge the orphanage, this enterprise costing $5,000. Later, two houses, on the same square with the

ST. MARY'S CATHOLIC CHURCH.

Sacred Heart School, were bequeathed to the parish for the benefit of the orphanage. Father Murphy has been a member of the Bishop's council since the organization of the diocese ; and he is also a permanent rector.

St. Mary's parish, with its splendid development, has no debt ; and, in point of organization, it is one of the best parishes in New England.

PAROCHIAL SCHOOLS.

St. Joseph's School, under the instruction of four Christian Brothers (Brother Jerome, superior), has 230 boys on its rolls, besides accommodating the younger girls who live in the northwestern part of the city and who are taught by two Sisters of Mercy. The school and the Brothers' house are on a splendid lot, the former building being well arranged, containing six class-rooms, and showing a brick basement and an open cupola.

REV. FATHER MURPHY.

The Sacred Heart School is located on Church street. Its lowest story is of brick, the other two being of wood. Its exterior is tastefully ornamented, the barocco work under the eaves being especially praiseworthy. It contains eleven rooms and a recitation hallway, every class having its own cloak-room. A parochial library is in this building. The school is heated by steam, is furnished with hot and cold air ventilators, and is well lighted. Fifteen Sisters of Mercy (Mother Fidelis, superior) from the Manchester mother-house, teach 415 girls, instructing also, up to the fourth grade, the boys who live in the southern section of the city. In the grammar grades history is treated topically, and diagram work is used in language analysis. A special course is given in vocal music. The high school curriculum, extending through three years, includes algebra, stenography, typewriting, literature, French, Church history, physics, civil government, and bookkeeping (single and double entry). Both schools are of the very first order.

SACRED HEART CONVENT.

The Sacred Heart Convent fronting on Central avenue, is bright and commodious, every Sister having her own room ; and it has a pretty chapel, furnished with stained-glass windows, a tasteful altar, and chaste frescoing.

The orphanage for girls is cared for by three Sisters of Mercy, and can be made to accommodate a hundred children. It is heated by steam, and is noticeable by reason of the neatness and sweetness of its dormitories. The orphans attend the Sisters' school.

The Central Avenue Baptist Church.

The church now known as the Central Avenue Baptist church, was constituted with thirteen members and recognized in the usual manner by a council on the twenty-third day of April, in the year of our Lord, one thousand eight hundred and twenty-eight. It was composed of persons who had been accustomed to worship with churches of the Baptist faith, but not finding those of their own belief and order in Dover, they took measures for the organization of a regular Baptist church. Of the thirteen persons who were active in this movement, seven were men and six were women. In March, 1828, Rev. Duncan Dunbar of New York was invited to preach to this body of Baptist friends, and as the result of a few Sundays' labor, three were baptized upon the profession of their faith. The first meetings of these brethren were held in the hall of a building which was attached to the block which now stands on Second street, familiarly known as the "Old Boarding House," and which once stood on the spot now occupied by the brick block known as the Morrill Block. The first pastor, Rev. Elijah Foster, was settled in October, 1829, and on the same day the present church edifice was dedicated to the worship of Almighty God, it having been erected largely by the arduous and persistent labors of the pastor with the cheerful co-operation of all the members of the church. It is worthy of remark, as indicating the labors of the pastor of that day, that on the first Sunday after the dedication of the church, he preached three sermons, baptized and gave the hand of fellowship to one new convert, administered the Lord's Supper and joined a couple in the bands of wedlock. Mr. Foster continued as pastor of the church till 1831, long enough to see it quite firmly established and increasing in numbers and spiritual strength through the faithful and earnest labors he made for it in its early days of weakness. From the year of its formation, now seventy years ago, to this present day, the church has maintained, through seasons of great trial as well as through seasons of great prosperity, a succession of godly ministers who have contributed their share to the advancement of this city in all good words and works, and as it looks back and reviews the past it can well thank God and take courage.

During the seventy years of the church's life, it has received into its fellowship nine hundred and twenty-two members. Its present membership is two hundred and forty-four, and its pastor is the Rev. W. H. S. Hascall, 4 Ham street.

CENTRAL AVENUE BAPTIST CHURCH.

REV. W. H. S. HASCALL.

W. H. S. Hascall is a native of Rutland County, Vermont, but while he was still a lad his father moved to Durham, Me., where he resides, though the boy spent much of his time in the city of Portland at the home of an uncle whose namesake he was. In addition to his other studies, he learned the printer's trade, and was called by the American Baptist Missionary Union to assist in their large Publishing House in Rangoon, Burma. He was soon transferred to the charge of the important station of Maulmain where the oversight of eighteen native churches, the direction of the evangelists and the supervision of several large schools, besides city and jungle preaching, devolved upon him. After eight years he returned to the United States for a period of rest, for a time serving as pastor of the Baptist church in Farmington, Me.

He returned with his family to Burma in 1883 and took charge of the Henzada mission until the British occupation of Upper Burma, when he was asked to found a new station in that dangerous locality. Land was purchased, mission buildings erected and a small church gathered, when he was obliged on account of the severe illness of his entire family to relinquish his work and return to America. After spending a year in resting and giving missionary addresses in various parts of the country he accepted a call to Fall River, Mass., where he remained six and one half years; from thence coming to Dover in October, 1896.

REV. W. H. S. HASCALL.

St. Thomas' Episcopal Church.

The first services in Dover in accordance with the doctrine and ritual of the Protestant Episcopal church of America were held by Rev. Henry Blackaller of St. Paul's church, Great Falls in Feb., 1832. The permanent establishment of this church in Dover is not due entirely to or chiefly, however, to the efforts of Mr. Blackaller, but rather to the Rev. Thomas R. Lambert, D. D., who in 1839

began the regular services of the church in what was then Belknap school, a wooden building then situated on Church street. On Sept. 2, 1839, gentlemen interested in the formation of a church met in this schoolhouse and entered into an association for this purpose. On Dec. 1, 1839, Rev. William Horton, before rector of Trinity church, Saco, became rector of St. Thomas' church. In 1840 a lot of land was bought on what is now the corner of Central avenue and St. Thomas st. A church building was erected and finished January, 1841, at the cost of $5800. The first service was held in the new church January 17, 1841. The church was consecrated by Bishop Griswold, March 17, 1841. In Aug., 1841, the parish consisted of sixty families and forty communicants. Rev. Mr. Horton resigned his rectorship Nov. 10, 1847. The Rev. Thomas G. Salter became rector Dec. 12, 1847. In 1860 gas was put into the church and the church bell was hung. On July 1, 1861, Mr. Salter resigned his rectorship and Sept. 1, 1861, Rev. Edward M. Gushee became the rector. During our late civil war Mr. Gushee was chaplain of the Ninth New Hampshire Regiment, and in his absence Rev. Charles Wingate officiated as rector. Mr. Gushee resigned in April, 1864. On Dec. 1, 1864, the Rev. John W. Clark became the rector, but resigned Sept. 16, 1866. The following February, Rev. George G. Field was chosen rector. Mr. Field resigned Aug. 16, 1868. Rev. John B. Richmond became rector Nov. 8, 1868. During the rectorship of Mr. Richmond the church building was altered inside and out, and its seating capacity increased. Mr. Richmond resigned April 29, 1876, and the present incumbent, the Rev. Ithamar W. Beard was chosen rector and entered upon his duties Nov. 5, 1876.

REV. ITHAMAR W. BEARD.

Ithamar Warren Beard was born in Pittsfield, N. H., Feb. 23, 1840. He fitted for college at the Lowell public schools, the Brimmer school in Boston, the Lawrence academy in Groton, Mass., and the Cambridge High school from which he was graduated in 1858. He entered Harvard college the same year and was graduated in the class of 1862. During the civil war he was lieutenant in the 19th Mass. Reg., but was obliged to resign his position on account of his father's failing health. He studied law in the office of D. S. and G. F. Richardson, Lowell, Mass., and was admitted to the bar of Middlesex county, Oct. 17, 1864. He was Secretary of the State Mutual Fire Insurance Company, Boston, in 1865. He practiced law in Lowell in 1866. He was Register of Deeds in Lowell in 1867 and was reelected in 1870. Dec. 1st, 1869, he married Marcy Foster of Nashua.

REV. ITHAMAR W. BEARD.

ST. THOMAS' EPISCOPAL CHURCH.

He was baptized by the Rev. Theodore Edson, D. D., of Lowell, March 25th, 1866. He was confirmed by the Rt. Rev. Manton Easttrom, D. D., April 5th, 1866. He was President of the Lowell Y. M. C. A. the first two years of its existence. He was graduated B. E. from the Cambridge Theological school June 18th, 1873. He was ordained Deacon by the Rt. Rev. Henry Vealy, D.D., June 15th, 1873. He was ordained Priest by the Rt. Rev. B. H. Paddock, D.D., June 21, 1874. He was rector of St. James church, South Groveland, Mass., from July 28th, 1873, to Nov. 1st, 1876. He was rector of St. Thomas' church from Nov. 1st, 1876, to the present date and he is still the rector. He has been a member of the Dover School Board, is chaplain of Moses Paul Lodge, Senior Pastor of the city, presiding officer of the Ministers' Association, a delegate to the general convention of his own church and he has been chaplain of the County Farm for ten years and more.

The old church occupied the northeast corner of the present site of the

City Hall and faced on Central avenue. This building was of wood and was torn down in 1891 and the new stone church was built. The new church was opened for use the first Sunday in September, 1892. Wm. H. Ward of Lowell was the contractor for the mason work, Tibbetts & Clark for. the carpenter work, Henry Vaughan, Boston, was the architect.

Washington Street Freewill Baptist Church.

The Washington street church was organized February 4, 1840, with thirteen members, most of them having been members of the First Freewill Baptist church, organized seven years before. For nine months meetings and Sunday-school were held every Sabbath in a small upper room at No. 246 Central avenue, with preaching part of the time. The first pastor was settled in November and the congregation so increased that the Sabbath meetings were soon removed to the Belknap schoolhouse, then on Church street and afterwards to the Court House.

The first house of worship was built in connection with an office for the publication of the *Morning Star* at a cost of $1600, and was dedicated September 21, 1843. The church then changed its name from Central street to Washington street and the number of its members was one hundred and fifty. The vestry, partly under ground, was afterwards finished and occupied for twenty years, and then abandoned as it was damp and unhealthful. In 1852 the house was enlarged, and the next year an organ was purchased at $800.

The printing establishment needed enlarged accommodations, and the church sold its interest in the house and held its last service there January 26, 1868. A large brick edifice was erected, at a cost of $24,000, its vestries were occupied in the autumn, and the house was dedicated October 28, 1869. The payment of its debt was completed in April, 1882, but on the morning of May 2d a fire in an adjoining building extended to the church and in one hour all was in ruins. In the afternoon a terrific wind blew in a part of the standing wall, burying five persons, four of whom were taken out badly injured and one was instantly killed.

WASHINGTON STREET FREEWILL BAPTIST CHURCH.

Sympathy was kindly offered, and the Belknap church, being without a pastor, tendered the use of its house, which was gratefully accepted and occupied till December 24, when the vestries were completed, and the audience room was dedicated March 22, 1883. The cost of rebuilding was $13,000, including the cost of the organ, which was $1300. The debt incurred by the rebuilding was bravely carried by the church until 1893, when the church received $1000 by bequest from the estate of Robert Cristie. By faithful effort and noble sacrifice over $2000 was raised among its friends and on Feb. 4th, 1896, they gathered in the church to witness the burning of the mortgage. Since then all pews have been free, and the running expenses of the church have been met by freewill offering.

The church is thoroughly evangelical in its spirit and methods, loyal to the Free Baptist faith and doctrine, and a firm supporter of denominational benevolences. In Oct., 1897, there were 170 resident members of the church and 58 non-resident making the total membership, 228.

REV. R. E GILKEY.

sor Co., Vermont, March 21st, 1857. He is the son of John and Ann T. (Currier) Gilkey. He was brought up on a farm where he had the advantages of a common school education. At the age of eighteen he entered Lyndon Institute, Lyndon Centre, Vt., to prepare for college. In the fall of '77 he entered Bates College, Lewiston, Me., graduating in '81. For three years he worked as a druggist, one year in Audubon, Iowa, and two years in Saco, Me. He then entered Cobb Divinity School in Lewiston, Me., graduating in 1887. He has held four pastorates. The first of one year in New Gloucester, Maine, the second of two years in the Corliss Street church, Bath, Me., the third of four years in the Brown church,

FRIENDS MEETING HOUSE.

REV. R. E. GILKEY.

R. E. Gilkey was born in Sharon, Windsor Co.,

Richmond, Me. He entered upon the labors of the fourth and present pastorate May 1st, '92.

Society of Friends.

The first mention we find of any Quakers in Dover is in 1662 when three traveling sisters were whipped out of town by order of Major Walderne. Dr. Belknap remarks in his " History of New Hampshire " that the Friends once comprised a third part of the population of the town. Their numbers now are quite respectable. The first " meeting " of Friends in Dover was established at Dover Neck as early as 1680, where their first meeting-house was built prior to the year 1700. It stood about half a mile north of the one built by the First Parish two hundred years ago, and was taken down about the year 1770. The one now occupied by the society was erected about the same time. Previous to this, however, they had a small house on Silver street, which was built prior to 1720, for it appears by their records that in December of that year they " agreed to repair their house at Cocheco." This house stood where the residence of Jacob K. Purington now stands. At that time they held meetings at Dover Neck as well as at Cocheco. The first "Monthly Meeting" was set up in 1702, and this record extends back to that time. The first " Quarterly Meeting" was established in 1708.

Advent Christian Church.

The Advent Christian church was or-

ADVENT CHRISTIAN CHURCH.

ganized May 4, 1881, by a body of Christians who had worshipped in houses and halls since 1843, having been literally without a resting-place during that period. At a meeting of the society and its friends in the spring of 1881, George E. Durgin, John Brooks and William H. Vickery were appointed to contract for the building of a house of worship.

It was built from the plans and under the direction of George Brown, the architect, at a cost of $5000. The seats are free and the church is supported by free-will offerings. The building contains an audience-room, 36 x 48 feet, and a vestry in the basement. The house was dedicated April 16, 1882, by a sermon preached by Elder John Couch, of Lawrence, Mass.

The First Unitarian Society of Christians in Dover.

The first meeting for forming this society was held Aug. 28, 1827, the society being organized on the 4th of September following.

The first meeting for public worship was holden at the Court House, Nov. 4, of the same year, when Rev. Henry Ware, Jr., then pastor of the New Brick church, Hanover street, Boston, and afterwards Professor of Pulpit Eloquence in Cambridge Divinity school, officiated. The house was built of brick in the year 1828, situated on Locust street and cost $12000. It was dedicated and Rev. Samuel Kirkland Lothrop ordained Feb. 17, 1829.

FIRST UNITARIAN CHURCH.

square feet, stood two houses, one of which he moved away, converting the other to rectory uses at an additional expense of $1200.

Father Richard began building St. Charles' Church May 1, 1896, and said the first Mass therein on the eighth day of the following November. The church cost, to build, $9400, the fittings and furnishings running the total expense up to $12,000.

REV. JULIAN J. RICHARD.

Father Richard was born at St. Maurice, P. Q., March 24, 1856, studied at the college and seminary of Three Rivers, and was ordained Sept. 19, 1880, by Bishop Laflesche, for the diocese of Three Rivers. For seven years after ordination he was a professor in the

The dedicatory services were performed by Rev. Dr. Nichols, of Portland, and ordination sermon by Rev. Dr. Parker, of Portland. The church was gathered the evening previous.

St. Charles Roman Catholic Church.

The parish of St. Charles, consisting of the French-Canadians of Dover, was organized in 1893. Rev. Julian J. Richard was appointed first pastor, Nov. 5, of the same year, saying Mass the following Sunday in Lowell Hall, where he officiated regularly. Aug. 17, 1894, he bought, for $6500, a fine lot on the corner of Third and Grove streets. On this property, which contains 10,000

ST. CHARLES CATHOLIC CHURCH.

college of Three Rivers, afterwards spending a year on duty at the cathedral. He came to the diocese of Manchester June 23, 1888, and was thereupon stationed at St. Augustine's, Manchester, where he remained until April 17, 1890, when he was transferred to St. Mary's Church, in the same city. April 3, 1893, he was made administrator of St. Francis Xavier's Church in Nashua, the pastor being in Europe. From the latter city he came to Dover.

Young Men's Christian Association.

The Dover Young Men's Christian Association was organized in 1888 and first occupied rooms in Ham's Block on Washington street. Soon after the increased membership demanded larger quarters and the association moved to Odd Fellows' Block. In December, 1896, the new Union Block was completed, the entire second floor of which was fitted up for the Association, with reading and recreation rooms, parlors, a well equipped gymnasium, with baths, and a hall with seating capacity of about two hundred. The rooms are open every week day from 9 A. M. to 10 P. M. and on Sunday afternoons, and the strange young man from out of town always receives a cordial welcome. Through its reading-room, library, mock-congress, camera club, gymnasium, pleasant, social life, religious services, the Association seeks to elevate men, mentally, physically and morally. Membership is open to all young men of good moral character. At the present time the Association has a membership of nearly 200 with officers as follows:

President, William C. Ogden: Treasurer, Frank E. Garside; Recording Secretary, Burton T. Scales; Auditor, Ernest B. Folsom; and Board of Directors, Chas. E. Cate, Rev. W. H. S. Hascall, Alfred E. Faye, Frank E. Meserve, E. H. Frost, T. M. Henderson, H. H. Burley, E. A. Crawford; E. B. Read, General Secretary.

Rev. James Thurston.

Rev. James Thurston is of the seventh generation from the common ancestor of the Thurstons of New England—Daniel Thurston, who immigrated to old Newbury, Mass., in 1635.

He was born in Buxton, York County, Maine, March 12, 1816. His parents removed to Danville, now Auburn, Me.,when he was quite young. His early life was spent on the farm and he enjoyed such educational advantages as were found in the country common schools of that day. He subsequently completed a course of studies in the Maine Wesleyan Seminary at Readfield, Me. He commenced his career as a minister of the Methodist Episcopal church in 1838 and remained in that work in Maine when he was "transferred" by the venerable Bishop Hedding to the New Hampshire conference.

REV. JAMES THURSTON.

His first appointment in New Hampshire was at Portsmouth in 1848. He has served some of the principal churches in the state and had two terms as Presiding Elder. He has twice been chosen as delegate by his brethren to the general conference.

He was appointed as pastor of the church in this city in 1869 and served two years when he was disabled by nervous prostration. During all the period of his ministerial life he preached twice on every Sabbath and often three times. He never had the benefit of a vacation, which was something quite unknown in those days. In all the earlier years of his service he received but a meager compensation for his labors. He was married in 1840 to Miss Clara A. Flint of Lubec, Me., who was always a most worthy helper in all his labor. She died in 1890. Mr. Thurston has made Dover his home for nearly thirty years, and is now the oldest resident clergyman in our city. He has served the New Hampshire Legislature as chaplain two terms, the only minister who had that distinction. He was a member of the House of Representatives in 1885, from Ward two in this city and a member of the constitutional convention in 1889, serving as chaplain to that body. He has performed such ministerial service as his strength would allow, having been a Class Leader and Trustee of St. John's church. He has acted as correspondent for several newspapers. He is a member of Strafford Lodge of Free Masons and an honorary member of St. Paul Commandery Knights Templar. He is the oldest Mason in this vicinity, having been made one in 1844. In politics he is a conservative Republican.

HARRISON HALEY.

Harrison Haley.

Harrison Haley is a son of John and Sally (Butler) Haley and was born at Lee. He received his education in the schools of Lee, Newmarket and Portsmouth. Upon leaving school he entered his brother's grocery store at Newmarket as clerk and later accepted a position as salesman in a dry goods store at Lowell. In the fall of 1849 he came to Dover and opened a dry goods store in which business he continued until the fall of 1870 when he was chosen cashier of the Cocheco National Bank, which position he has since filled. Mr. Haley has ever been most active in the various enterprises of the city, always ready to do his part to promote any cause that was for the good of our citizens. His public spiritedness and perseverance have been manifest in many of the public enterprises of Dover. Through his energetic efforts a street railway was built, adding considerably to the convenience of the public. The introduction of the City Water Works, the establishment of a Children's Home and a Home for Aged People are among the movements which engaged his interest and zeal. The erection of an Observatory on Garrison Hill from which thousands of people have greatly enjoyed the grand views, was also an enterprise of his. He has been a member of the City Government and of the Board

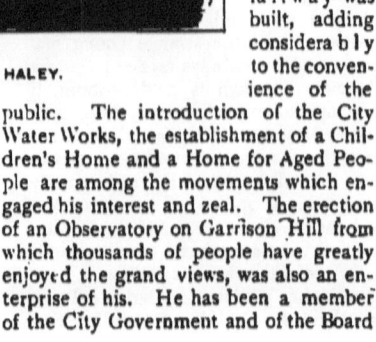

of Education. In religious persuasion he is a Methodist and has been for seventeen years Superintendent of the St. John's Methodist Episcopal Sunday-school.

Hon. Charles H. Sawyer.

Charles Henry Sawyer was born in Watertown, N. Y., March 30, 1840. He is eldest son of Jonathan and Martha (Perkins) Sawyer. His ancestry on both the paternal and maternal sides were among the early settlers of Massachusetts. He attended the schools of Watertown until he was ten years of age, when the family removed to Dover, and he completed his education in this city. He entered the Sawyer Woolen Mills at the age of seventeen, the plant then being engaged in the manufacture of flannels. He had become thoroughly proficient in the business

HON. CHARLES H. SAWYER.

at the age of twenty-six and was then appointed Superintendent of the Mills. In 1881 he became President of the company and since then the general management of the mills has been in his hands. Throughout his business career Mr. Sawyer has been markedly successful. He has held many public offices. He served in both branches of the City Councils, was Representative to the Legislature in 1860-'76-'77, a member of the staff of Governor Charles H. Bell in 1881, and in 1884 he

was delegate to the National Republican Convention in Chicago. In 1886 he was elected Governor of New Hampshire, and during his term of office he represented the state in many centennial celebrations that were held during that period, particularly at Philadelphia on the occasion of the celebration of the one hundredth anniversary of the promulgation of the Constitution of the United States. Another centennial was that in New York of the inauguration of President Washington. Mr. Sawyer is a Director of the Strafford National Bank, a Trustee and Vice-President of the Strafford Savings Bank and a Director of the Dover Gas Light Company. He has held the positions of President of the Dover Horse Railroad Company, Director and Executive Member of the Granite State Insurance Company, President of the Elliot Bridge Company, a Director of the Dover and Portsmouth, the Dover, Great Falls and Conway, and the Wolfeboro Branch Railroads. He is a member of the Congregational Society of Dover. He is a Mason and has been twice chosen Master of the lodge and for many years was Eminent Commander of St. Paul Commandery, Knights Templar. Mr. Sawyer was married February 8, 1865, to Susan Ellen, daughter of Dr. James W. and Elizabeth Cowan of this city. Their children are, William Davis, who married Susan Gertrude, daughter of Hon. Joshua G. Hall; Charles Francis, who married Gertrude Child, daughter of Hon. Henry W. Severance of San Francisco; James Cowan, who married Mary Pepperell, daughter of Judge George Seward Frost; and Edward and Elizabeth Coffin Sawyer.

The Dover Clothing Company.

The Dover Clothing Company was established in 1880 and has built up a bus-

WINFIELD S. BRADLEY.

iness which is remarkable alike for its magnitude and scope. The company's popularity lies in the fact that all classes of trade are catered to with equal care and ability. They will make you as choice a custom garment as any tailor in New England, and they will furnish you with a strong, durable garment at a very low price, for working wear. Their custom made garments are absolutely correct in fit, style and finish and the assortment of patterns kept in stock embraces all the well known cloths, woolens and cas-

DOVER CLOTHING COMPANY'S STORE (INTERIOR).

simeres manufactured by the Sawyer Woolen Mills.

Mr. W. S. Bradley, the proprietor of this representative establishment, is a native of Fairfield, Vt., and is widely and favorably known in business circles throughout this section of the state. He gives close supervision to the various departments of the undertaking, and has the business thoroughly systematized. From six to ten assistants are employed in the store, and from twenty-five to fifty in the workrooms, thus assuring prompt attention to the needs of patrons. The premises comprise two floors

CHARLES E. HODSDON.

sisting of a heavy stock of ready to wear clothing, hats, caps, and all the latest fashionable novelties in gentlemen's furnishings.

Since the opening of this establishment it has met with splendid success on account of the unusually fine stock of goods carried and the excellent and refined taste shown in their selection.

Charles E. Hodsdon.

Charles E. Hodsdon was born and educated in Dover. At the age of fourteen years he entered the store of C. E. Bacon to learn the jewelry business and served eleven years perfecting

INTERIOR HODSDON JEWELRY STORE.

and a basement at 436-438 Central avenue and are well adapted for displaying the excellent stock of goods carried, con-

himself in its every detail. Ten years ago Mr. Hodsdon opened a modest store in the vicinity of the Democrat office, and at the time occupied by Alexander Frazier. Six months later he moved into his present magnificent store in the National Block, 444 Central avenue. The premises are excellently fitted up, the furnishings benig of a substantial nature. Handsome plate-glass show cases show to perfection the rare assortment of cut and uncut gems and precious stones, diamonds, solid gold rings, watches, chains, and ornaments all tastefully arranged and bearing evidence of the splen-did patronage the store en-joys from the best class of our citizens and those of the surround-ing towns. Mr. Hodsdon also carries a line of rare art pot-tery, solid sil-ver and silver-plated w a r e and an exten-sive line of gold and silver watches and chains, silver toilet articles, bronzes, onyx and marble c l o c k s, cut glass, specta-cles, bric-a-b r a c, etc. Special atten-tion is devo-ted to watch and jewelry repairing and the mounting of gems. Everything carried in stock is of an exceptionally fine quality suitable for the most fastidious class of customers. Mr. George R. Hodsdon, a graduate of the Bucklins School of Optics of New York, who has been constantly associated with Mr. Charles E. Hodsdon, is in charge of the optical and engraving departments. He makes a specialty of fitting spectacles for weak or defective sight.

In addition to his jewelry business, Mr. Hodsdon conducts one of the largest retail bicycle stores in the state, handling the Stearns, Victor, Waverly, Lovell Dia-mond and other high class wheels. In the rear of the store are the workshops where every class of repair is attended to by skilled workmen at short notice.

Hon. Joshua G. Hall.

Joshua Gil-man Hall is a lineal descen-dant of Dea-con John Hall, who lived on the land now cultivated by John Wesley Clements on Dover Neck. The Hall spring which has been known by that name for over two hundred years is on the C l e m e n t s farm near the river. It has been used by m a n and beast s i n c e the day that Deacon Hall discovered it. On the ma-ternal s i d e Mr. Hall is descended f r o m Capt. Jeremiah Gil-man of Wakefield, who was one of Stark's officers at Bennington, having raised a company for the campaign when over sixty years of age. Report says he was the first man in the fight after Gen. Stark who led the column.

Mr. Hall is the son of Joshua G. and Betsy (Plummer) Hall of Wakefield, where he was born Nov. 5, 1828. He gradu-ated at Dartmouth college in July, 1851,

HON. JOSHUA GILMAN HALL.

and was admitted to the bar in 1855. Since 1857 he has resided in Dover. His public services have been practically continuous from June, 1862, to March 4, 1881, having been Solicitor for the County of Strafford from June, 1862 to June, 1874; Mayor of Dover, 1866, 1867; City Solicitor, 1868, 1869; member New Hampshire Senate 1871-'72; Representative to New Hampshire Legislature, 1874; Attorney of the United States for the district of New Hampshire from April, 1874, to Feb., 1879; elected to the forty-sixth Congress and re-elected to the forty-seventh as a Republican, receiving 16,310 votes against 15,047 for John W. Sanborn of Wakefield. In these various offices he has been diligent in the discharge of his public duties and the confidence of his fellow citizens has been shown by continued advancement. He is a deacon in the First Parish Congregational church in Dover of which his ancestor, John Hall, was first deacon, and where, in the words of the old Dover records for the year 1671, he "agried with the selectmen to sweep the Meeting-House and ring the bell for one hole yier & to have for that serves the sum of ten pounds." On Nov. 16, 1861, he was united in marriage to Miss Susan Elizabeth Bigelow of Boston, Mass. Their children have been Grace Bigelow, who married Wm. H. Cook of Florida, Susan Gertrude, who married Gen. William D. Sawyer of Dover, and a son, Dwight Hale, who graduated at Dartmouth College 1894 and was admitted to the bar in 1897.

Mr. Hall died Oct. 31, 1898.

Gen. William Davis Sawyer.

William Davis Sawyer was born November 22, 1866. He is the eldest son of Hon. Charles H. and Susan Ellen (Cowan) Sawyer. General Sawyer was educated in the public schools and graduated from the Phillips Academy, Andover, in 1885. He pursued his studies at Yale University and received the degree of A. B. from that institution in 1889, immediately taking up a bus-

GEN. WILLIAM D. SAWYER.

iness career in connection with the Sawyer Woolen Mills, in which he has held the responsible position of Treasurer since 1891. Gen. Sawyer is a Director of the Portsmouth & Dover R. R. and was Quartermaster General on the staff of Governor John B. Smith, with the rank of Brigadier General. He has always taken a deep interest in politics and has been a delegate to the Republican National Convention of 1896, member of the committee to notify President McKinley of his nomination, member of the Republican State Committee since 1890 and of the Executive Committee of same in 1896. Gen. Sawyer is also a member of Moses Paul Lodge No. 96 A. F. and A. M., Belknap Chapter, Royal Arch Masons, Orphan Council, St. Paul Commandery, Knights Templar, and of the Amoskeag Veterans of Manchester. He is also a member of the following clubs: Bellamy Club, Dover; Derryfield Club, Manchester; Piscataqua Yacht Club, Kittery; University, Yale and Wool Clubs of New York city. Gen. Sawyer married Susan Gertrude, daughter of Hon. Joshua G. Hall and has two children, Jonathan and Elizabeth Bigelow.

Charles Henry Fish.

Charles H. Fish, Agent of the Cocheco Manufacturing Company, was born in Taunton, Mass., a son of Captain F. L. and Mary (Jarvis) Fish. After receiving his education Mr. Fish entered the machine shops of the Amoskeag Manufacturing Company in Manchester, and from that time has been actively engaged in manufacturing. He was appointed agent of the Cocheco Company's Mills and Print Works September 1st, 1895, succeeding Mr. John Holland.

Colonel George H. Peirce.

Colonel George H. Peirce was a native of this city, where he was born February 15, 1829, and always had his home. Educated among us, early identifying himself with the business interests of Dover, growing with its growth, and always actively interested with whatever in his view tended to its prosperity and progress, few men became better known, and few acquired and retained through life a wider personal popularity and influence. A man of generous impulses, liberal and open-hearted, not without his faults, but possessing many marked excellencies and sterling traits of character. Possessed of excellent judgment, great energy, and rare business qualifications, he was a thoroughly active, enterprising and progressive man. In his opinions he was outspoken, and no one ever had reason to doubt his position on any question. Nevertheless he retained the regard of those whom he opposed, and seldom lost his friends while continually drawing new ones around him.

From his early youth he was actively engaged in business, commencing in partnership with his brother, Andrew Peirce, now of St. Louis, and the late Thomas Stackpole of this city, as wholesale merchant on Dover Landing, and

CHARLES H. FISH.

afterwards continuing the firm with Elisha Jewett, of South Berwick, Me. His attention, however, was early called to railroad construction, in which he first engaged, as early as 1850, on the extension of the Cocheco Railroad from Farmington to Alton Bay. In 1852, in company with Elisha Jewett and William Flynn, he took a large contract on the Southbridge and Blackstone Railroad, now a part of the Air Line from New York to Boston; and about the same time he became engaged in the Saratoga and Sackett's Harbor Road, running largely through the wilderness of Northern New York. He afterwards became interested in many large contracts on various roads, including among others the Fall River and Newport, the extension of the Concord & Portsmouth to Manchester, the Little Rock and Fort Smith, Ark. Railway, the extension of the Boston

COLONEL GEORGE H. PEIRCE.

& Maine to Portland, and the Portsmouth and Dover. In the last two he had as partners Messrs. Flynn and Charles B. Gardner of this city. Colonel Peirce's largest contract was for the construction of the European and North American, at a cost of $7,500,000. He subsequently sold out his interest in this. He had nearly completed the Portsmouth & Dover road at the time of his decease, Sept.

13, 1873. Had he lived he would undoubtedly have had the contract for the Great Falls and Conway extension from Great Falls to Dover. In politics Colonel Peirce was always a Democrat, yet he often voted independently and never blindly followed party dictation in the support of bad nominations. He was twice the candidate of his party for Railroad Commissioner, running ahead of his party in both elections. He also represented Ward 3, in which there was an anti-Democratic majority of 162—a result that was due in part to his well-known views on railroad questions identified with the prosperity of Dover, but altogether more to his great personal popularity.

— • —

Charles Francis Sawyer.

Charles Francis Sawyer, second son of Charles H. and Susan E. (Cowan) Sawyer, was born in Dover Jan. 16th, 1869. He was educated in the Dover public schools, at Phillips Academy, Andover, Mass., and Yale University. He entered the employ of the Sawyer Woolen Mills in 1889 and is now superintendent and director of that company, has served in both branches of the Dover City Government, also in the New Hampshire National Guard as 2nd Lieutenant of Company D, 1st Regiment and Captain and

Commissary on the Brigade Commander's staff. He is a member of the First Parish (Congregational) church, also a member of Moses Paul Lodge, Belknap Chapter, Orphan Council, and St. Paul Commandery K. T.; is a Past Eminent Commander of St. Paul Commandery and is at present an officer in the Grand Commandery of New Hampshire. Mr. Sawyer is a member of Dover Grange and of the Bellamy Club. He married Jan. 29th, 1 8 9 5, Gertrude Child, daughter of Hon. H. W. Severance of San Francisco.

Granite State Park.

Granite State Park was purchased in the spring of 1896 from the Strafford County Agricultural Society by Frank A. Christie for Hon. Frank Jones. Mr. Jones is President of the Granite State Park Association and is also largely interested in the Readville and Rigby tracks.

CHARLES FRANCIS SAWYER.

In May of the same year Mr. Christie began making improvements. Two feet of thoroughly ground and fine-screened loam was spread on the track which is now such that horses and colts can be worked out without any possibility of getting sore feet. Three hundred new horse sheds have been built providing the most excellent conveniences for the stabling of horses. A steel water tower 93 feet high with a tank holding 30,000 gal-

lons of water has been erected, thus ensuring a plentiful supply of pure water which is conveyed throughout the Park by means of four inch pipes. Mr. Jones has also remodeled and enlarged a capacious house within the park and has furnished and equipped it as a first-class hotel and clubhouse. The Park Tavern as it has been named, has become most popular with horsemen and its success is assured. It is lighted by electricity and heated by steam throughout and every attention is paid to the requirements of owners and trainers of horses.

The first race meeting was held in August, 1897. On the first day it was used, Gentry went a mile over it in 2.04 3-4, the last half in 1.01. The Horse Review, in speaking of the horse "Gazette," says: "Last season he paced a succession of staunch and game races. At Portland, Me., August 20, he won a great six-heat contest, taking the last three heats in 2.11 1-4, 2.09 1-4, 2.10 1-4, beating seven horses. This he followed up by a wonderful eight-heat victory at Dover, beating the pacing queen Lottie Loraine, and four others in a tremendous contest, and taking the third, fourth and eighth heats in 2.09, 2.10 1-2, 2.10 3-4. His eighth heat in 2.10 3-4, driven by Tom Marsh at Dover, stands as the best on

GRANITE STATE PARK.

record. In this race Lottie Loraine paced a mile in 2.07 3-4, which was at that time within one second of the world's record for mares." Marion Mills paced a mile over this track in 2.06 1-4. The track measures 7 inches over a mile, and has one of the finest hub rails of any track in the country.

Granite State Park is without doubt to-day, all points considered, the best mile track in the world over which to condition and race horses. There is a decided change in the grade of each quarter which is thought very desirable for conditioning horses. The roads in four different directions are perfect for road work. The track is on high land bordering on a beautiful sheet of water known as "Willands Pond." Frank A. Christie, the Treasurer and Manager of the Association, has done much to bring about the present excellent state of affairs. He has worked indefatigably to make the track as near perfection as possible, and the success which has attended his capable management is best evidenced by the large list of entries at each meeting.

Directed by an executive staff embodying experience, energy and wealth, with a track having a record as one of the fastest in the land the association has acquired a reputation which they will al-

ways sustain. The purses are generous, and the conduct of its affairs, the results of its gatherings, the importance of the events, and the interest attending them together with the achievements upon the speedy and magnificent one mile track are guarantees of the honorable and progressive management which is characteristic of Hon. Frank Jones in all his affairs.

HOWARD GRAY.

Howard Gray.

Howard Gray, Superintendent of the Cocheco Manufacturing Company's Print Works, was born at Dorchester, Mass. In 1883 he became connected with the Merrimack Print Works at Lowell, Mass., and spent thirteen years there learning the business in all its branches. He came to Dover in 1895 to enter the employment of the Cocheco Manufacturing Company and was appointed Superintendent of their Print Works in February, 1896.

John Drowne.

John Drowne, Superintendent of the Cocheco Manufacturing Company's Mills, was born at Eaton, N.H., and received his education at the district and high schools of his native town. At the age of eighteen he enlisted in the Eighteenth New Hampshire Regiment and saw service with the Ninth Army Corps in front of Petersburg. In July, 1865, at the close of the war, he received an honorable discharge. The following year he entered the employment of the Atlantic Cotton Mills at Lawrence, Mass., where he remained until 1869 when he went to Houston, Texas, to start the weaving in the Houston Mills. A year later he returned to the Atlantic Mills at Lawrence and remained until 1874 when he went to New Hartford, Conn. In 1876 he entered the service of the Wamsutta Mills, New Bedford, remaining until 1880 when he returned to New Hartford Conn., as Superintendent of Greenwood Company's Mills. He came to Dover in March, 1896, as Superintendent of the Cocheco Company's Mills, a position which he has since most capably filled.

Mr. Drowne is a Thirty-Second Degree Mason, Lafayette Consistory, Bridgeport, Conn., a member of Amos Beecher Lodge No. 121, New Hartford, Conn., and of Washington Commandery, Knights Templar, Hartford, Conn. He is also prominently associated with the I. O. O. F., being a member of Monadnock Lodge, No. 145, Lawrence, Mass., and of Annawam Encampment No. 8, New Bedford,

Mass. He is a member of Charles W. Sawyer Post, G. A. R., Dover.

Arioch Wentworth.

Arioch Wentworth was born in Rollinsford, just beyond the Dover boundary, June 13, 1813. He is the son of Bartholomew and Nancy (Hall) Wentworth and a direct descendant of Elder William from whom have sprung the Colonial Governors of New Hampshire and the other illustrious men who bear that name. Elder William came to Dover from England in 1639 and his ancestry can be traced back to the year 1066, when William the Conqueror subdued England. Mr. Wentworth was born in the old homestead which was granted to Elder William 250 years ago and still remains in possession of the family. He received his early education in the schools at Dover and Rollinsford and at the age of fourteen attended the Franklin Academy, spending five winter terms acquiring knowledge. In the summer months he worked on his father's farm. Although urged by his father to prepare for college he decided to go to Boston. He felt a craving for a broader life with larger opportunities and carried out his determination. He was fortunate in securing work in a granite

JOHN DROWNE.

yard. Subsequently he went to work in a soapstone factory and received good pay. He was temperate and frugal, and having saved a little money went home in the fall, and added a little to it by teaching school through the winter.

He returned to Boston in the spring, leased the place which belonged to Mr. Blunt, his former employer, who had failed, worked energetically and entered upon and prosecuted with vigor the soapstone business, then new and untried. He succeeded and made money. He had mechanical genius, industry, temperance, and economy and devoted his time to a fast growing business. Mr. Wentworth not only had health and good habits but had a quick and clear insight into machinery. He invented or improved many of the machines, tools and processes he had to use in his business and thus nearly doubled his profits.

Mr. Wentworth next took on the marble business and imported and worked about all the foreign and domestic marbles, 300 men being employed in his yard. He kept increasing the business until it became the largest and most important marble works in Boston. Even in his early days he foresaw the development and destiny of the city of Boston,

ARIOCH WENTWORTH.

and rightly judged that property could not decline in a city of such promise, and already the literary and commercial metropolis of New England. And so he began at an early day to invest in real estate in Boston. His first purchase was a $3,000 dwelling house and he subsequently purchased land for his business which then covered an acre of ground.

As fast as his money accumulated he invested it in real estate and held and improved it. He has never lost faith in real estate and today he is the largest real estate holder and pays the largest city tax of anyone in Boston who earned his own money.

Mr. Wentworth has circumnavigated the globe. He has crossed the Atlantic several times and with his family has visited the principal continental cities of Europe. Part of a winter he spent in Egypt going up the Nile and visiting all the ruins and inspecting the antiquities of that historic land. When he was over eighty years of age he started with his family, five in all, for a tour of the world, via San Francisco, Japan, China and the principal countries and cities of Asia, returning via the Red Sea and Suez Canal, visiting Rome and from thence through Europe to England, sailing from Liverpool home. Mr. Wentworth saw nothing in his travels to compare with our own country which he terms "God's Country," and declares there is no other like it.

Mr. Wentworth has shown by his actions that his heart is alive to early associations and friends. The Wentworth Home for the Aged, erected within a rifle-shot of his old homestead is a lasting monument to his munificent charity. He has donated $30,000 to this purpose alone and has also liberally endowed out of his abundance th· Children's Home. These institutions receive extended notice in another part of this work.

It may be truly said that Mr. Wentworth is a benefactor of his race. He is a ready giver to those private charities which enlist so deeply the sympathies of true men. He gives cheerfully and without ostentation and this has sometimes led him to veil a generosity of

GEORGE E. SCHULTZ.

character and a tenderness of feeling which are among his most striking traits. He is one of the firmest of friends, and one of the most thoroughly honest and upright of men. Well may we be proud to claim such a man as a citizen and future generations will remember and revere the name of him who has done so much to ameliorate the sufferings of the virtuous poor and solace the declining years of our aged and impecunious citizens.

George E. Schultz.

George E. Schultz was born in Alsace, Germany, coming to this country when six years of age. Upon completing his education he entered the laboratory of the Eddystone Print Works near Philadelphia and learned textile printing and coloring. While gaining a practical knowledge of the business he studied chemistry under private tuition and at the Philadelphia College of Pharmacy. While occupying a responsible position at Eddystone, he, in 1894, accepted the appointment of chemist at the Cocheco Print Works and was shortly afterwards promoted to the position of colorist.

George R. Smith, M.D.

George R. Smith, M. D., was born at Barnard, Vt., July 7, 1859, the son of Rufus B. and Mary J. Smith. He was educated in the public schools of Gaysville, Vt., and prepared for college at Goddard Seminary, Barre, Vt. He entered Tufts College, class of '84 and studied medicine at the Hahnemann Medical College, Chicago, graduating with the class of '88, and receiving his degree of M. D. from that institution. Dr. Smith began the practice of his profession in Dover in June, 1888, opening an office at 378 Central Avenue, but upon the completion of the Masonic Temple he removed his office to the present handsome suite of rooms in that building, where he has since remained. His patients have grown yearly more numerous, and his standing among his professional associates has been annually enhanced. In the community Dr. Smith stands high. He is a member of the New Hampshire Homœopathic Medical Society, the National Society of Electro-Therapeutics, Moses Paul Lodge, A. F. and A. M., St. Paul Commandery, Knights Templar, and of the Knights of Pythias. His time has been freely given in reply to public demands and the alleviation of disease and suffering. Dr. Smith is still in the prime of life and for him the future presents inspiring views of hope crowned with the reward that follows faithful, meritorious work in any line of life.

DR. GEORGE R. SMITH.

I. B. Williams & Sons.

In their line of production there is probably no other concern in the country so well and favorably known, and none whose products are in more universal use and demand throughout the United States, Canada and

RESIDENCE OF DR. GEORGE R. SMITH.

Europe than I. B. Williams & Sons.
Their leather belting, strapping and
lace leather have attained a world-
wide reputation and the various
brands of the firm are everywhere
recognized as the highest standard
of quality.

The foundation of the present
business was laid by the senior
partner, Isaac B. Williams, in 1842.
At that time the business was confined to the manufacture of belting
for the Cocheco Manufacturing Co.
and the workshops of the concern
were located in the Cocheco Mills.
In 1871 Frank B. Williams was admitted to partnership with his father
and the firm became I. B. Williams
& Son. From its inception the industry prospered. The attention
of manufacturers was attracted to
the superior quality of belting
turned out by the firm and the demand for their products became so
great that in 1874 it became neces-

FRANK B. WILLIAMS.

sary to acquire more commodious
premises to meet the demands of
the trade. A large and valuable
property on Orchard Street was purchased and was added to and remodeled so as to afford the desired
facilities. George H. Williams was
taken into partnership in 1878, the
style of the firm then becoming as
at present, I. B. Williams & Sons.

In 1882 the premises were found
to be wholly inadequate for the ever
increasing output and the factory
was torn down and entirely rebuilt
on a much larger scale. The firm
purchased an adjoining property
and erected a substantial four story
brick building, with a tower five
stories high, containing elevators,
stairways, etc. Ten years later, in
1892, another four story brick building was added, and in 1896 this was
supplemented by another two story
building and a separate boiler house
measuring 40 x 50 feet. The factory
faces on Orchard street, with an ell,

GEORGE H. WILLIAMS.

BIRD'S-EYE VIEW OF I. B. WILLIAMS & SONS' FACTORY.

having a frontage of 100 feet and on Waldron street of 165 feet.

The motive power is supplied by two 200 horse power upright boilers and one 225 horse power Corliss engine thus insuring abundant power for the various machines operated. The first floor of the factory is occupied by offices and the shipping department, on Orchard street. In the rear of the same is the modern machinery for the tanning of lace leather and currying of leather. The second story is occupied by the superintendent's office, store room for finished lace leather,

the new Washington light and is steam heated throughout. Sanitation and ventilation are carefully looked after and each room is lightsome and kept in excellent order. None but thoroughly skilled mechanics are employed in all departments.

The output of the factory is as follows: 1000 to 1200 butts weekly, which is manufactured into leather belting. Three tons of shoulders daily, which are curried and worked into stock for Goodyear inner soling, saddle flaps, welting leather and strapping and from 1200 to 1500

CURRYING DEPARTMENT.

lace finishing room, belt stretching room, straightening room, and rough leather room. The entire third floor of the building is occupied by the belting and strapping departments; the fourth floor by the lace drying rooms, belting and leather stuffing and drying rooms.

The mechanical equipment of the factory is of the highest order. Every device and machine looking toward perfection in the production of leather belting lace leather, Goodyear inner soling, strapping, welting, etc., is utilized. The building is lighted by gas, electricity and by

hides per week are tanned and worked into lace leather. In January, 1883, the firm commenced the manufacture of tanned and raw hide lace leather in a small way, and its superiority over other makes soon became apparent by the increased demand. Their raw hide lace gave such good satisfaction the firm decided that some distinguishing mark or pattern would be of advantage and adopted the trade mark "Cocheco." They speedily began to feel the benefit of this, consumers all over the country called for Cocheco lace, and their trade

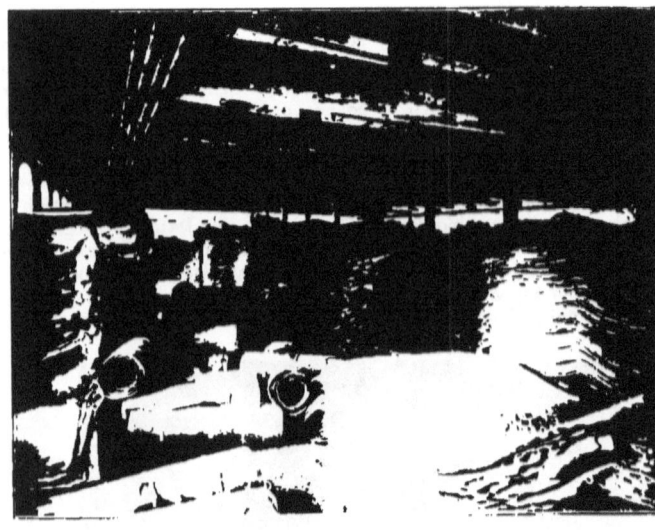

ROUGH LEATHER ROOM.

stock and extra heavy. For use in cotton, woolen, paper, pulp and saw mills and for main drivers it has no equal. The next grade Short Lap is made from the same quality stock only a little lighter in weight.

commenced to double from year to year until today Cochero lace has the widest and best reputation of any raw hide lace on the market, and is more extensively used. The firm now makes several times as much lace as the next largest concern in the country. In addition to side lace they manufacture and sell millions of feet of cut raw hide lace every year.

The Cocheco Short Lap belting is unexcelled, being made from pure white oak bark tanned

Superior, Defiance, Buckeye, Cairo. Special Light Double, Light Double and Gilt Edge Solid Round Belting, constitute the other grades made by this firm, with one exception, Dynamo. This last mentioned belt, as its name in-

SECTION OF BELT ROOM.

dicates, is for use in driving electric light machinery and is of special construction, being made of the choicest pure oak tanned leather, thoroughly stretched, water-proofed and nothing but center stock is used in its construction. This brand of belting is known all over the country for its superior excellence in dura-

BELT ROOM LOOKING SOUTH.

bility, steady and true running qualities. They are also one of the largest manufacturers of Solid Round Belting in the country, the goods being of the highest quality.

The productions of the factory are sold not only all over this country but a considerable export business is done with Europe, Australia, China, and Japan. The firm has a large store in Chicago for the distribution of its goods throughout the northwest, also a smaller one at Cleveland, while agencies are established in all the important cities in the Union. A competent corps of traveling salesmen are employed, covering the north, east, south and west.

No similar house in the country occupies a more promising position in the commerce of the country and with every advantage that large facilities, ample

SECTION OF BELT ROOM.

res)urces and experienced management can provide,its future growth and advancement may confidently be predicted to be fully in accord with its past record of usefulness and influence.

Hon. James E. Lothrop.

James Elbridge Lothrop, son of Daniel and Sophia (Horne) Lothrop was born in Rochester Nov. 30, 1826. His first American ancestor, on his father's side, Mark Lothrop, was younger brother of Rev. John Lothrop the first minister of Scituate, Mass., and grandson of John Lowthorpe, of Lowthorpe, Yorkshire, England. Mark was in Salem, Mass., in 1643, but removed to Duxbury, and thence to Bridgewater in 1656, where he died in 1686. His grandson, Mark, married Hannah Alden, a great-granddaughter of John Alden, of the *Mayflower,* by his wife, Priscilla Mullins, commemorated in history and in Longfellow's charming poem. The one who said, "Why not speak for yourself, John?" was the direct ancestress of James E. Lothrop. On the maternal side, Dr. Lothrop is descended from William Horne, of Horne's Hill in Dover, who held his exposed position in the Indian wars, and whose estate has been in the family name from 1662 until the present generation ; but he was killed in the massacre of June 28, 1689. Through the Horne line, also, came descent from Rev. Joseph Hull, minister at Durham in 1662, a graduate at the university of

HON. JAMES E. LOTHROP.

Cambridge, England ; from John Ham, of Dover ; from the emigrant John Heard, and others of like vigorous stock. It was his ancestress, Elizabeth (Hull) Heard, whom the old historians call a " brave gentlewoman," held her garrison-house, the frontier fort in Dover in the Indian wars, and successfully defended it in the massacre of June 28, 1689.

Dr. Lothrop received his education at the Rochester Academy, and at Strafford Academy, Dover, and taught school at the age of sixteen.

In 1843 he took up the study of medicine with his uncle, Jeremiah Horne, M.D., at Fall River, and also acquired a practical knowledge of the drug business in his uncle's drug store. At the age of nineteen he came to Dover and engaged in the drug business, subsequently admitting his brothers, Daniel and John C., into partnership, under the style of D. Lothrop & Co. Drug stores were opened at Newmarket, Meredith Village, Great Falls and Amesbury Mills, Mass. These were afterwards sold and the business became concentrated in Dover. Dr. Lothrop took the degree of M. D. at Jefferson Medical College in 1848, but relinquished his practice of medicine to devote his entire attention to the drug business. So largely had the business grown that it was necessary to increase the working force and a half interest in the drug store was conveyed to Mr. Alonzo T. Pinkham, the firm name becoming Lothrop & Pinkham. The firm of D. Lothrop & Co. next engaged in the clothing business, admitting their father, Daniel Lothrop, into partnership, under the style of D. Lothrop & Sons, and established branches at Rochester and Great Falls, now the city of Somersworth. That at Rochester was sold out and the firm purchased the clothing business of Joshua Varney which was removed to the home store on Franklin square. The death of Daniel Lothrop, senior, occurred in the year 1872, and a brother, M. Henry Lothrop (at one time President of the Dover Common Council), after eight years' service as salesman, in 1877 took one half interest in the clothing business, D. Lothrop & Co. retaining the other half. Since 1870 they have been in the new, lofty, spacious store which forms the centre of Morrill's block. In 1880, M. Henry Lothrop was transferred to the Boston department and the firm entered into partnership with Charles H. Farnham & Co., who took one third interest in the clothing business, under the firm name of Lothrops, Farnham & Co.

To the Dover business was also added in 1873 another department, consisting of musical instruments, music, pianos and organs, sewing machines and musical merchandise, which has since grown to immense proportions, being now one of the largest houses of the kind in the state. The name of D. Lothrop & Co. has even more than a national reputation. In 1850 they purchased the stock of books held by Elijah Wadleigh and began business as booksellers. In 1852 they purchased the entire building. In addition to their retail business they built up a good jobbing trade, and did some publishing. In a few years they sold the Dover book business and Daniel Lothrop went to Boston and opened a store—D. Lothrop & Co.—at Cornhill. This was a success and in 1876 they took the whole four story double store on Franklin street corner of Hawley and fitted it elegantly. The great success of their publishing work necessitated the leasing of a five-story building on Purchase street for manufacturing purposes.

The sudden decease of Daniel Lothrop in 1892 left the whole control and management of the immense publishing business in the hands of Dr. J. E. Lothrop and Mrs. Daniel Lothrop, and it was ably conducted by them for about two years. In the meantime the whole business and property of D. Lothrop & Co. had been purchased by Dr. J. E. Lothrop, including the drug and music stores and real estate (John C. Lothrop afterwards repurchasing the property at Great Falls). These were of such magnitude and importance that with his increasing years Dr. Lothrop deemed it wise, even with great pecuniary sacrifice to reorganize the D. Lothrop Co. corporation, and with the consent and assistance of Mrs. Daniel Lothrop and John C. Lothrop a new corporation was established in 1894 under the style of the Lothrop Publishing Co., with the condition that it should conduct business upon the same principles and carry out the purpose and designs of the founders. By adopting this course he has been relieved of the enormous labor attending the personal conduct of the Boston business and is enabled to add greater force and vigor to all his Dover enterprises.

Dr. Lothrop has in addition to his business the entire care of real estate, comprising many stores and tenements, including the Morrill estate. He has been a director in the Cochecho National bank from 1858, was chosen Vice-President in 1873, and has been its President since 1876. In 1871 he became a director in the Cocheco Aqueduct Association, its clerk in 1872, and from 1875 its president. He was also a director in the Portsmouth and Dover R. R., in the Eliot Bridge Company, has been President of the Dover Board of Trade. In 1872, Dr. Lothrop represented the city in the Legislature and served two terms, 1883-1884, as Mayor of the city. He married Mary E., daughter of the late Joseph Morrill. In politics he is a Republican, and his religious persuasion is that of a Methodist.

In promoting all manufacturing and industrial interests he has always taken a most prominent, active, unselfish and successful part, and the general manufacturing and mercantile interests of the city and state have been elevated and held at a higher standard by his indomitable energy, sterling integrity, untiring and persistent efforts and constant devotion to the public welfare. As a financier his judgment has been sound and his views of the most healthy character. As chief magistrate of the city and in the legislature his influence was ever used in behalf of progressive enterprise and judicious expenditure. It is to his endeavors that the Dover Public Library

music trade, none enjoy a higher reputation than the Oliver Ditson Company of Boston. Dr. J. E. Lothrop has for several years been associated with this company in the sale of pianos, in New Hampshire and Massachusetts, in connection with his large music store. The warerooms of J. E. Lothrop & Co. are in the Morrill block and are conveniently appointed. They contain a complete assortment of pianos and organs and an excellent line of mandolins, banjos, guitars, violins,

CLOTHING DEPARTMENT, LOTHROPS, FARNHAM & CO.

owes its origin. Now in his seventy-second year, after fifty-three years devoted to business, he is active in body, clear and vigorous in mind and successfully conducting enterprises in this city, Somersworth and Rochester of a magnitude and importance, the labors and responsibilities of which few even younger men would be willing to assume.

——— • ———

James E. Lothrop & Co.

———

Of those who devote attention to the

music boxes, reed instruments and in fact everything usually associated with a first class music store. A large stock of musical merchandise is always to be found here, including sheet music, music books and musical instrument fittings. All the latest popular songs are put on sale as soon as published. The celebrated Butterick's patterns are also kept in stock. In the department of second hand pianos and organs may be found an excellent and varied lot of second hand instruments, which will either be sold at mod-

LOTHROPS, FARNHAM & CO.'S STORES, MORRILL BLOCK.

erate prices or rented subject to purchase. In the sewing machine department will be found all the standard makes of new and second hand machines, containing all the latest styles and most modern improvements. On account of taking other machines in exchange for the celebrated New Home, a large number of various makes are constantly for sale at merely nominal prices. The trade of the house is large and extends generally throughout this state and Massachusetts and patrons

Daniel Lothrop & Sons in 1855 and continued so until 1872 when, upon the death of Daniel Lothrop, Senior, the name was changed to D. Lothrop & Co. In 1883, Charles H. Farnham became a partner, the style becoming Lothrops, Farnham & Co. The premises occupy a splendid position in the Morrill block, two handsome stores being utilized for the purposes of the business. Branches are maintained at Rochester and Somersworth. The Rochester store was opened in April, 1886, and the

SHOE DEPARTMENT, LOTHROPS, FARNHAM & CO.

are assured of receiving every advantage of quality and price when dealing with this representative concern.

Lothrops, Farnham & Co.

The house of Lothrops, Farnham & Co. has contributed in a most important way to the material prosperity of Dover. Its resources are ample and it leads in its line of trade throughout a large amount of territory. The business was established by Dr. James E. Lothrop under the name of

Somersworth store in Aug., 1895. In all thirty-one courteous and thoroughly competent salesmen are employed. They carry at all times a vast and seasonable stock of clothing in all grades, stylish in cut, of excellent make and finish, neat, substantial, and sold at remarkably low prices. In the hat and furnishing goods department the display is always a tempting one, comprising all that is desirable in shirts, collars, cuffs, neckwear, underwear, hosiery, gloves, bags, hats, caps, etc. The shoe department is replete with all the latest standard makes of shoes for both sexes and a large stock of children's and misses' footwear is kept on hand. This department will bear favorable comparison with any store of the kind in New England, being elegantly furnished and carpeted. It is safe to assert that a more comprehensive, elegant or desirable assortment of goods appropriate to the various departments cannot be found in the state. The store itself is the handsomest and one of the largest in the city, perfect-

Somersworth and Boston, pushing with vigor the interests of the firm.

Lothrops & Pinkham.

For over half a century the name of Dr. Lothrop has been associated with the drug business in Dover. It was he who, in 1845, established the concern from which has sprung the present large business. The firm at its inception was D. Lothrop & Co., but in 1868 it became

FURNISHING GOODS DEPARTMENT, LOTHROPS, FARNHAM & CO.

ly lighted and ventilated and is a pleasant place to visit. Polite and obliging salesmen give the same attention to rich and poor alike and the prices of all the goods are uniformly low. Built upon a solid foundation with no misrepresentation the firm has worthily earned the reputation of reliable outfitters and hopes to still further augment its trade by constantly studying the wants of their patrons. Mr. Farnham is the active partner and manages the entire business. He spends one day each week in Rochester,

necessary to add to the working force and Mr. Alonzo T. Pinkham was given a half interest. From the very start the business was a success. In 1870 the store, which is located in the Morrill block, was enlarged and now measures 25 x 75 feet with about 1000 feet of cellar space. In compliance with the popular demand the firm added a wall paper department which has become a leading feature of the house. The store is well and tastefully fitted up with large plate-glass show cases and cabinets, and complete stocks are carried of the freshest and purest drugs and chemicals, articles for the toilet, fancy goods, soaps and perfumes of domestic and foreign manufacture, cigars, druggists' sundries, etc. A specialty is made of compounding family recipes and physicians' prescriptions with accuracy and care, only the purest drugs being used. Pure soda and mineral waters are dispensed, all syrups being the choicest the market affords. Mr. Pinkham is a thoroughly expert pharmacist and is held in high esteem by his fellow professionals and the community at large. Several assistants are employed and patrons are at all times assured of receiving courteous and prompt attention. In 1888 the Wheeler store at the corner of Central avenue and Silver

AUREN W. HAYES.

it was moved across the street into a building especially constructed for it, where under the efficient management of Mr. Geo. F. McFarland a successful business has been established.

— . —

A. W. Hayes.

Mr. A. W. Hayes was born in South Newmarket in 1852 and as a boy attended the district school of his native town. He came to Dover in 1868 and entered the employment of James A. Horne (jeweler), in September, 1869, to learn the watchmaking business, remaining until February, 1874. During this period he had worked assiduously to master his chosen calling in which he soon became an expert, and upon leaving Mr. Horne he accepted employ-

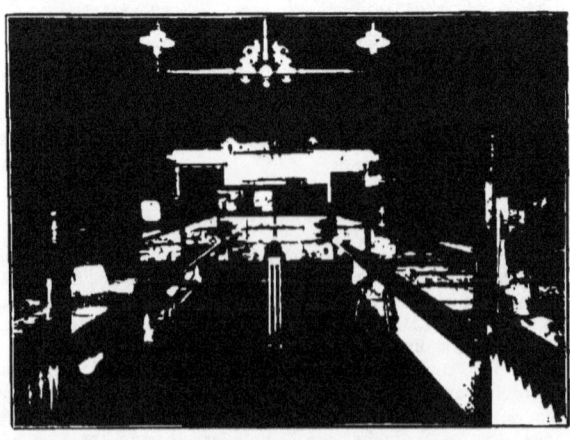

A. W. HAYES' JEWELRY STORE.

street, was purchased and thoroughly refitted and stocked as a modern pharmacy, meeting with such success that in 1894

ment as watchmaker with the large and well known jewelry firm of Charles W. Kennard & Co. of Boston, where he remained for ten years. In 1884 he returned to Dover and purchased the jewelry business conducted by C. S. Kingman at 424 Central avenue. The store is tastefully appointed, fitted with handsome plate-glass show windows and possesses every facility for displaying to the best advantage the magnificent and valuable stock. This embraces fine American and European watches, diamonds and precious stones, both mounted and loose, jewelry, sterling silver and silver plate, clocks, bronzes, art novelties, and many articles of use and ornament, all of which have

quality. Mr. Hayes is most popular with his fellow citizens and is a member of Moses Paul Lodge of Masons and of Wecohamet Lodge, Order of Odd Fellows. He was also parish clerk of the Peirce Memorial church three years. In addition to his jewelry business Mr. Hayes makes a specialty of handling standard makes of bicycles, including the celebrated Sterling and Orient wheels. In this department a large business is done and every facility is afforded patrons to acquire a wheel that will stand the test of time.

BYRON F. HAYES' STORE.

been selected with a refined taste and judgment that meet with the approval of all customers. A watch and jewelry repairing department is among the facilities of the house, and the most costly watch may be confidently left here with the assurance that it will be returned in perfect running order. Mr. Hayes has devoted a lifetime to the jewelry business, is practically proficient in all its details, and is fully conversant with the requirements of patrons. He is progressive in his methods to secure the choicest goods and supply them at as low prices as is consistent with

Byron F. Hayes.

This house was originally founded by Ira W. Nute & Co. in 1872. In 1879 Mr. Byron F. Hayes became manager and in 1887 entered the firm as a partner, the style being changed to Nute & Hayes. Mr. Hayes continued as the managing partner of the firm until Mr. Nute's death in March, 1896. Three months later he acquired the business and has since conducted it under his own name. The store is located in the Morrill block and has ample accommodation for the reception of customers and for displaying the large and costly stock which is always kept on hand. This embraces everything in the way of staple and fancy dry goods and notions, ladies' and children's furnishings, underwear, hosiery, gloves, corsets, skirts, waists, ladies', misses' and children's garments and everything associated with a first class store of the kind. A specialty is made of fine imported dress goods, silks, velvets, cloaks, capes and suits, all of the latest styles and fashion. The house caters to no particular class, but provides for all and quotes prices which will compare favorably with any similar concern in the

BYRON F. HAYES.

large cities. All goods are carefully selected and are the products of the leading manufacturers of the country.

Mr. Hayes is a native of Milton, where he was born Nov. 30, 1854, coming to Dover in 1872 and entering the employment of Ira W. Nute & Co. He is conversant with the dry goods business in all its details and has conducted the affairs of his house with judgment and vigor, advancing the interests of his customers in every legitimate manner, and at the same time developing a business that is most creditable. He is a member

of the I. O. O. F. and of the Royal Arcanum. Mr. Hayes was married November 30, 1887, to Miss Mary F. Whitehouse of this city and has a charming residence at 28 Mount Vernon street. He is a member of the Methodist church and of the Official Board of that body.

Daniel H. Wendell.

The subject of this sketch was born in Dover July 25, 1814, and resided in this city during a long and useful life, departing on Dec. 26, 1895. Mr. Wendell's ancestry dates back to 1640 when Evart Jansen Wendell emigrated from Germany to this country and settled in Albany, N. Y. This ancestor had three sons, Abraham, Isaac and Jacob. One of these remained in Albany, another removed to Portsmouth, N. H., and a third to Boston. The subject of this sketch came from the Boston branch, and numbered among his relationships Wendell Phillips and Oliver Wendell Holmes. Mr. Wendell's occupation was principally that of insurance agent and manager of real estate, and in this field he built up a large and prosperous business. He was also Justice of the Peace, Insurance Commissioner and member of the Legislature prior to the city charter.

Mr. Wendell was married on Sept. 16, 1837, to Huldah Jenness, daughter of Deacon Solomon Jenness. Of their children, three lived to maturity, one son and two daughters. The son, D. A. Wendell, M. D., died in 1871, from a disease contracted in the civil war, throughout which he served as an assistant surgeon. One daughter, Ellen E., died in 1874, while the remaining daughter, Caroline R., survives.

Mrs. Wendell, the wife and mother, was a woman of great intellectuality, with a strong grasp of affairs, and was always intent on doing the utmost possible good in her journey through life. Very philanthropic, her charities were many and varied. Her death in 1885 was a sad blow to her family and friends. Miss Caroline R. Wendell, the surviving daughter, has been President of the Woman's Christian Temperance Union since 1892, and previous to that time for thirteen years was secretary of the same institution. She is also connected with several other philanthropic institutions of a similar character. Miss Wendell's efforts in behalf of temperance and purity have been very marked and she is an active influence for good in her chosen calling.

Mr. Wendell may be said to have grown up with Dover. He was familiar with its scenes from early boyhood and his reminiscences of old Dover were the delight of family and friends. He could relate by the hour the various changes time has wrought in the physical aspects of this ancient town and his remembrance of occurrences and men of 60 to 70 years ago was very vivid.

He was a man of marked individuality, with firm convictions and the courage to express them. Perhaps the most notable feature of his life, however, was his high regard for integrity. He was a practical example of the fact that business can be conducted successfully and with honor. His benevolence was large but discriminating and much of it found its way through the hands of his family in the upbuilding of the cause of temperance and the rights of woman. His bearing upon the street was striking and attractive. Courteous in demeanor with lithe step and graceful yet dignified carriage, he reminded one

DANIEL H. WENDELL.

of a gentleman of the old school. Intensely devoted to his family, kindly in his nature, with strong religious convictions, he has passed away with a firm belief that God had a strong hold upon him and the future, and that He would adjust all things well.

Charles L. Howe.

Charles L. Howe belongs to one of the oldest and most honored families of New England. He is a son of the late Dr. A. W. Howe whose mother was sister to Ex-Governor Levi Woodbury of New Hampshire, and is a direct descendant on the maternal side of President Dunster, the first president of Harvard College, appointed in 1638. It was in President Dunster's house that the first printing press used in the Western hemisphere was set up, being used in those early days to print the college pamphlets.

Mr. Howe's love for flowers began in his early childhood, and even then he was the proud possessor of lovely plants. He embarked in the nursery business when he was quite young, the present being the third set of greenhouses he has owned. Mr. Howe sold out his business in Nashua in 1891 and came to Dover, having purchased the site until

A CITY HALL GROUP.

then occupied by Henry Johnson, whose greenhouses had been entirely destroyed by fire. Mr. Howe rebuilt them on a larger and more elaborate plan and two years later upon his marriage to Miss Nellie A. Vittum, daughter of Mr. B. F. Vittum, he erected his present fine residence adjoining the conservatories.

The entire plant has been constantly enlarged and improved until it is today the largest establishment of its kind in the state. There are twelve large glass-houses covering an area of nearly an acre of ground, the entire nursery occupying over five acres. The nurseries are on the slope of Garrison Hill facing the south and are particularly well adapted

tablished under the style of Tilton & Hanson, remained so until March last when Mr. Frank W. Hanson became the sole proprietor. The salesrooms are elegantly and attractively appointed and the stock carried embraces all the most stylish goods of both home and foreign production required by gentlemen, and includes fine neckwear, collars, dress and negligee shirts and all of the many indispensable articles which make up the wardrobe of a well-dressed and refined man. While Mr. Hanson has always made it a point to provide all the latest novelties and goods of the kind in the market for the most exacting and discriminating customers, he has with com-

CHARLES L. HOWE'S NURSERY.

to the requirements of the business. Every description of ornamental trees and flowering shrubs are cultivated and in the greenhouses the most exquisite and delicate flowers are grown the year round. Mr. Howe makes a specialty of floral designs for weddings and funerals, his trade extending throughout all eastern New England. In the summer fifteen gardeners are employed, including one of the most expert landscape gardeners in New England. Six delivery teams are necessary to distribute the products grown.

Frank W. Hanson.

The clothing business originally es-

mendable enterprise provided for the requirements of the masses, by carrying a complete stock of medium grade goods at popular prices. A specialty is made of gentlemen's, youths' and juvenile clothing which cannot be surpassed for excellence both as to style and quality. Those desiring custom-made garments can have their needs attended to promptly and have a wide range of materials from which to select. All goods are procured direct from the manufacturers and have a reputation for novelty, variety, high character and tasteful selection, while the prices are based on liberal and fair dealing methods. The premises are centrally located in the Masonic Temple, the store running from Central avenue to Locust street, on both of which thoroughfares there are entrances. The trade of the house, while largely among the citizens of Dover, is by no means wholly confined to this city, but extends to the surrounding cities and towns.

Mr. Hanson was born August 1st, 1865, at Charlestown, this state, and came to Dover when three years old. He received his education at the public schools and afterwards graduated from the Bryant & Stratton Commercial School, Boston. Altogether he has spent fourteen years in the clothing and

FRANK W. HANSON.

Farnham & Co. Mr. Hanson is progressive and enterprising and is ably assisted in his business by a competent and courteous staff of assistants.

J. H. Randlett.

The carriage business founded by Mr. Randlett in 1864 and its subsequent prosperous development has been commensurate with the enterprising activity and superior skill which have ever characterized its management. Mr. Randlett is a native of Lee, and in the early fifties went to California where he remained seven years. Upon his return to the east he engaged in business in Newmar-

INTERIOR FRANK W. HANSON'S STORE.

furnishing business, ten of which were passed in the employment of Lothrop,

ket, coming to Dover to found the present business in 1864. At that time the premises were located on Locust street, but the ever increasing volume of business demanded larger premises and facilities and two years later the present commodious quarters in the old Belleview Hall on Central avenue were acquired and remodeled to suit the requirements of the business. Mr. Randlett is an expert in all the branches of his vocation of a carriagemaker and as he personally oversees all the labors of his assistants he is enabled to secure the most satisfactory results. The factory is eligibly located and is equipped with all the necessary tools and appliances that can contribute to the production of the most efficient, stylish and reliable work. Thirty highly skilled mechanics are employed in the several departments, and the range of production embraces fine carriages of every description, wagons and sleighs. These are all constructed of the best and most thoroughly seasoned woods and the standard makes of steel and iron, while the upholstering, trimming, painting and general finish could not be surpassed for style and elegance. They are unexcelled for strength, durability, soundness of every individual part, ease of draught, fineness o finish and beauty of appearance. A ful stock is carried, special attention is given to order work and the prices are as low as is compatible with the highest class of materials and workmanship. The trade of the house is throughout New England principally, but orders are constantly received from every part of the Union. Mr. Randlett has been elected twice as representative, serving two terms in the legislature and also two years in the Common Council.

J. H. RANDLETT.

RANDLETT'S CARRIAGE FACTORY.

Alfred Chase Faye.

Mr. Faye was chosen to his present position of principal of the Dover High school from among a large list of worthy candidates two years ago, coming here from Chillicothe, Ohio. From the first, the interest of the new principal in the school and in the city has been deep and sincere. He is a thorough educator and to his credit may be placed a great portion of the praise for the high standing enjoyed by this time-honored institution during his incumbency of the office. Mr. Faye was born in Natick, Mass., April 4, 1867, and has taught school since he was seventeen years of age. Among the places where he has led the thought of youth are Marion, Wrentham and Quincy, Mass. He then entered Harvard college, where his standing as a student was very high and he graduated with honor. Upon leaving college the celebrated Lawrenceville school of Lawrenceville, N. J., made him a tempting offer and he remained at that institute for one year, from thence going to Chillicothe, Ohio. He spent two years there and it speaks well for the appreciation and esteem in which he was held that last year he was offered the superintendency of the Chillicothe public schools. He preferred, however, to remain in Dover and fortunate indeed was the city to retain in her service this able educator. Mr. Faye was also superintendent of the Sudbury, Mass., public schools. The principals of our High school have always been men of rare intelligence and possessed of more than usual educational abilities, able to impart instruction to our youth in such manner that they will retain the knowledge gained. Mr. Faye is no exception to the rule and his success and pleasing popularity with his pupils proves that his selection to this important position was a wise one. There are at present from 180 to 190 pupils of both sexes attending the school and two male and three female instructors are em-

ALFRED CHASE FAYE.

ployed under Mr. Faye's able guidance.

John B. Stevens.

Early in the century, John B. Stevens, senior, made Dover his permanent residence. He was of that ardent band of Dover abolitionists so much in evidence fifty years ago. His eldest son, the subject of this sketch, was born in Dover May 29, 1836. He was educated in the Dover High School, South Berwick Academy, Franklin Academy, New Hampton Literary Institute, and Comer's Commercial School. He taught school for a short time in 1856. He has always lived in Dover, except during a short residence in New York. From 1864 to 1894 he was City Clerk of Dover. In 1865 he was City Treasurer. He succeeded the Hon. Jeremiah Smith, as Trustee of the Dover Public Library in 1886 and acted as Secretary of the Trustees for four years. For many years he was prominently identified with the public school system of this city, being successively a member of the Prudential Committee of District No. 2; of the Superintending School Committee of the city; of the Board of Education, Board of Instruction and School Committee of the Consolidated City District; his vote and influence were ever for progress. No man did more, few as much to make possible our present system and methods. Our city High school, our graded schools, our superintendency, may all be traced to the period of Mr. Stevens' participation in school government, and to him more than to any other is due their existence at this time. He was an active member of the House of Representatives in 1897.

Mr. Stevens belongs to the B. P. O. E. and is a member and clerk of the Dover Sportsmen's Association. His literary contributions upon this subject have been extensive and have won for him among sportsmen more than a local reputation as an author. He has a very decided literary talent and is graphic in his description of places and events; clear and cogent in the presentation of his views and ideas, and possessed of a keen, discriminating literary taste which enables him to add grace and beauty to the strength and vigor of his writings.

He early foresaw the value and need of a pure and abundant water supply. He was identified with the movement

JOHN B. STEVENS.

started in 1887 in this direction and grasped the project in all its details at the outset, explaining and advocating the wisdom of the enterprise and ever using his influence with the official representatives of the citizens to enlist their support of the financial measures required in the carrying on of the work. The many resolutions, orders and contracts passed and accepted by the City Council and its committees, calling for large expenditures of money, were drafted or reviewed by him with such fidelity and skill that legal entanglements were avoided and the city treasury saved from revisionary measures and readjustments. The city of Dover owes much to him for this successful administration of the complex duties of the office of City Clerk and for his insistent method of doing things right. His present position on the Water Board fitly recognizes his ability to judge wisely, steer safely and act promptly, at all times in the interest of the city and for the protection of his fellow citizens.

Mr. Stevens has two sons of whom he may be justly proud. Col. Frank B. the elder, went through the Dover High school and Phillips academy, Exeter, and graduated from Yale College, thence entering the field of journalism as city editor of the Troy (N. Y.) Telegram. Later he was called to a desk in the Boston Globe Office, and is now conducting a successful advertising business of his own in Boston. He is a member of Governor Wolcott's staff with the rank of Colonel. Hermon W., the younger son, attended the common schools of Dover and Phillips Academy, Exeter, and then became a Harvard graduate, finishing his academic training at Heidelberg

University. He is now a writer in Boston.

Harris M. Shaw.

Harris M. Shaw was born at East Andover in 1854. He attended school at Gorham, Me., and when sixteen years of age went to Boston to learn the trade of a carpenter and builder. He returned to Dover in January, 1875, and the following year formed a partnership with William Beede, under the style of Beede and Shaw. Subsequently Mr. Pike was admitted a partner and the firm became Beede, Shaw and Pike. This firm built the Moulton shoe shop on Sixth street for a steam mill and carpenter shop. Mr. Shaw withdrew from the firm in 1883 and has since been engaged in general contracting and building at 16 Hough street, and from his advanced methods and the close personal attention given to all contracts he has succeeded in securing some of the most important building contracts for private residences in Dover and the surrounding towns. He completed the planning and remodeling of the house at the corner of Hough street and Central avenue, at present occupied by Dr. Blanchard, but a short time ago. Only skilled workmen are employed and the best materials used, and all work entrusted to him is carried out

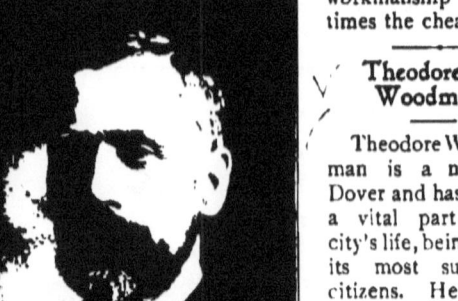

HARRIS M. SHAW.

under his own close personal supervision. Mr. Shaw also attends to general house repairing and contracts for every class of building work. His figures will always be found reasonable, being based upon the fundamental principle that the best workmanship is at all times the cheapest.

Theodore W. Woodman.

Theodore W. Woodman is a native of Dover and has become a vital part of the city's life, being among its most substantial citizens. He is a son of Samuel Woodman, of the Durham branch of the family, and Lydia E. (Rollins) Woodman, daughter of Captain James Rollins of Somersworth. From his parents he inherited habits of industry and prudence and has proved himself to be abundantly endowed with those sterling qualities which constitute the successful man. Mr. Woodman has always been an ardent believer in the value of real estate and no one in the city has done more towards its development. He has for many years been largely interested in realty. In 1898 he erected the imposing Woodman block at the corner of Central avenue and Hale street and has been instrumental in providing good tenements for the masses at low rentals. At the present time over one hundred tenants occupy his buildings and

RESIDENCE OF H. M. SHAW.

he well sustains the reputation he has acquired of being a just and liberal landlord.

During the civil war Mr. Woodman occupied a responsible position with the Freedman Bureau, under Gen. O. O. Howard at Washington, and had charge of a large number of men. He has devoted much of his time to public affairs, serving in various capacities in the interests of the city. He has been selectman, councilman and alderman of Ward 4, which he represented in the Legislature for four years. His entire legislative career

THEODORE W. WOODMAN.

was most acceptable to his constituents who frequently expressed their appreciation of his services. Mr. Woodman has also served on the Board of Education, has been President of the Board of Trade and of the Bellamy club, and was one of the incorporators and is now a trustee of the Wentworth Home for the Aged. He was also chairman of the Building Committee and it is largely owing to his foresight and clear judgment that this elegant building was erected at such a small outlay. He has been markedly successful in

WOODMAN BLOCK.

business and while still in the prime of life has acquired a competence. He owes his entire success to his business ability, application, perseverance and singleness of purpose. He is a man of many resources and shows what can be accomplished by enterprise, coupled with integrity and fair dealing. He is the surviving member of his branch of the Woodman family, his brothers, Charles S. and James R., and sister, Lizzie C. having deceased.

Tasker and Chesley.

There is probably no profession in which a greater delicacy of feeling is necessitated than in that of the funeral director. It is asserted that the above firm is possessed of all the necessary requisites to successfully carry on their business as funeral directors and embalmers. The firm was formed July 1, 1897, succeeding Mr. A. N. Ward. They are both energetic young men, thoroughly acquainted with the duties of their profession, and possess a courteous demeanor. Their rooms, located at 12-14 Third street, are fully stocked with high grade goods suitable for occasions where bereavement occurs,

H. B. TASKER.

meeting the requirements of all classes of patrons. They furnish everything requisite for funerals, are prompt in meeting their engagements and can always be implicitly relied upon in all matters relating to interments. They make a specialty of embalming and possess the necessary natural endowments, as well as the technical knowledge so peculiarly needful in this business. Mr. Tasker was born at Newmarket in 1870, receiving his education at the public schools. Upon leaving school he entered the undertaking business with his father and gained a thorough and practical knowledge of it. He came to Dover in 1897 to form the present partnership. He is a member of Rising Star Lodge, No. 47, A. F. and A. M. and of Pioneer Lodge, No. 1, K. of P., Newmarket. Mr. Chesley was born in 1869 at Hutchinson, Minn., but went to Newmarket at the age of twelve years. He received his education in the public schools and at the New Hampton Literary Institute. He was Town Treasurer of Newmarket for two years and is a member of Rising Star Lodge, No. 47, A. F. and A. M. and Pioneer Lodge, No. 1, K. of P., Newmarket.

T. T. CHESLEY.